The Night House Files

CLASSIFIED

THE NIGHT HOUSE FILES

THE WINTERMOOR LIGHTS

Dan Smith

Illustrated by
Luke Brookes

Barrington Stoke

Published by Barrington Stoke
An imprint of HarperCollins*Publishers*
1 Robroyston Gate, Glasgow, G33 1JN

www.barringtonstoke.co.uk

HarperCollins*Publishers*
Macken House, 39/40 Mayor Street Upper,
Dublin 1, DO1 C9W8, Ireland

First published in 2025

Text © 2025 Dan Smith
Illustrations © 2025 Luke Brookes
Cover design © 2025 HarperCollins*Publishers* Limited

The moral right of Dan Smith and Luke Brookes to be identified
as the author and illustrator of this work has been asserted in accordance
with the Copyright, Designs and Patents Act, 1988

ISBN 978-0-00-870050-8

10 9 8 7 6 5 4 3 2 1

This book is a work of fiction. Names, characters, places and incidents are products of the writer's imagination or used fictitiously. Any resemblance to actual people, living or dead, events or locales is entirely coincidental

All rights reserved. No part of this publication may be reproduced, stored in a retrieval system, or transmitted, in whole or in any part in any form or by any means, electronic, mechanical, photocopying, recording or otherwise without the prior permission in writing of the publisher and copyright owners

Without limiting the exclusive rights of any author, contributor or the publisher of this publication, any unauthorised use of this publication to train generative artificial intelligence (AI) technologies is expressly prohibited. HarperCollins also exercise their rights under Article 4(3) of the Digital Single Market Directive 2019/790 and expressly reserve this publication from the text and data mining exception

A catalogue record for this book is available from the British Library

Printed and bound by CPI Group (UK) Ltd, Croydon, CR0 4YY

MIX
Paper | Supporting
responsible forestry
FSC™ C007454

This book contains FSC™ certified paper and other controlled
sources to ensure responsible forest management.

For more information visit: www.harpercollins.co.uk/green

For the believers

The Night House Files

Officially, the Night House does not exist. But it is real. It is an old and secret organisation that investigates the truth behind strange events around the world; events that include the paranormal, the extra-terrestrial and the bizarre. Events that governments do not want you to know about. The findings of these investigations are filed and kept safe by a mysterious person known only as the Nightwatchman. Once a year, the Nightwatchman delivers a file to me. My job is to turn the contents of the file into a story so that you can know the truth. That is the Nightwatchman's wish, and I dare not disobey.

The following story is taken from File ET339: the Wintermoor Lights.

Everything you are about to read is true. The names of people and places have been altered to protect the innocent.

News article taken from the SATURDAY GAZETTE, dated 8th December 1984

What is wrong with the children?

On Friday this week, a dozen children failed to turn up for lessons at Wintermoor Comprehensive School. All of the children were in the Third Form, and most had never missed a day of school.

The mystery deepened when the school contacted the parents of the missing children only to be told that they had all set off as usual that morning.

A local resident describes the moment he found one of the children wandering along Reacher's Lane.

"I almost ran her over," Dave Johnson recalls. "I stopped to see if she was all right, but she just stared at me and babbled about being 'chosen' or something. Then she sort of snapped out of it and walked off like nothing had happened. Honestly, what is wrong with children these days?"

After a police search, all of the missing children were found unharmed in different locations around Wintermoor. According to reports, the children were behaving strangely when found. They seemed to be in a trance, and several of them were muttering incoherently.

A teacher from Wintermoor Comprehensive who wishes to remain anonymous said: "It's some kind of prank. It has to be. Some of the children even claim to have seen 'lights' in the sky over Wintermoor. I blame TV. They watch far too much rubbish these days."

Two Weeks Earlier

Saturday, 24th November 1984

Some stories are easy to tell. When I know exactly where to begin and exactly where to end. But this is not one of those stories. I have spent many hours staring out of my window, trying to decide how and when to begin. Forty years ago? Fifty? A *hundred*? Perhaps even longer than that. But 1984 is when everything came to a head in Wintermoor. It's the year that everyone remembers, even though it's the year they all want to forget. It's the year of the tragedy, so that's when I'll begin.

November 1984. When the lights came.

Zoe Bishop, fourteen years old, was the first to

see one. She had just come home from early morning swim training. It was still dark when her mum pulled onto the drive and switched off the car engine.

"We're home," she said, nudging Zoe, who was dozing in the passenger seat.

Beyond the warmth of the car interior, the pavements glistened with frost. A smattering of lonely snowflakes drifted into the halo of a streetlamp.

Zoe blinked hard and rubbed her eyes before opening the door and climbing out of the car. The cold air hit her straight away.

"Come on, darling – let's get you inside before you catch your death," her mum said.

Zoe turned her face to the clear sky, feeling the gentle touch of the snowflakes. And that was when she spotted the light hovering over the woods north of town. About a mile away. It was small and faint, but Zoe was transfixed. At first, she thought it was a star, but then she realised it was moving. Travelling quickly in a straight line towards her.

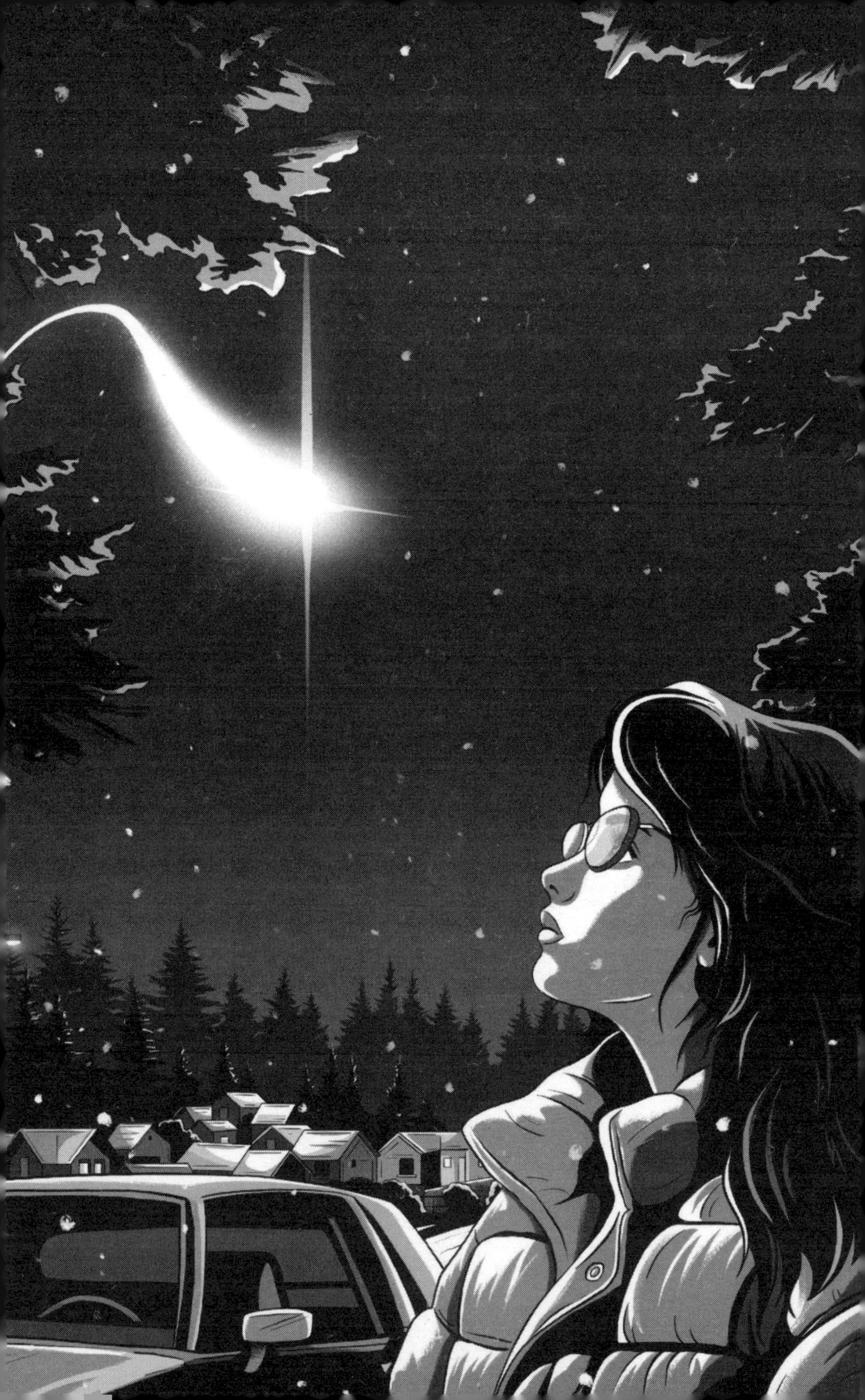

Zoe was aware of her mum walking up the path to the front door, jangling her keys. Zoe wanted to join her, to go inside where it was warm, but the light held her gaze, and she couldn't look away.

It approached over the roofs of the houses until it was directly above the place where Zoe was standing. Then it came to a sudden stop.

Zoe tipped her head right back to look up at it. Snowflakes settled on her eyeballs and melted there, but she didn't blink. She could see it clearly now, just a few metres above her. No larger than her fist, the ball of light twisted and rippled like living water. It floated in the air, impossible and mesmerising, pulsing all colours at once as it began to expand and contract in time with her breathing.

Zoe watched the light, transfixed, for what seemed like a long time, then it dropped towards her and disappeared.

REPORT: X5N846-1

CLASSIFIED

TOP SECRET

Interview with: Tara Fisher
Date: Friday, 9th January 1987

The following is taken from an interview with Tara Fisher, former best friend of Zoe Bishop, which took place two years after the incident at Wintermoor.

TARA FISHER: That's what Zoe told us about seeing the light. It was Saturday, and we were in Flynn's on the high street having hot chocolate. It's all in my diary. There was me, Jasmine and Dennis – whose real name was David. David Takagi. We called him Dennis cos his hair stuck up like Dennis the Menace from *The Beano*. Anyway, Zoe told us she saw this light in the sky, and Dennis got really into it. He read that weird magazine about monsters and UFOs and that. He was like, "It's aliens, or maybe ball lightning," but me and Jasmine just thought Zoe was winding us up. Like it was a joke or something. So we teased her a bit, and she got really whazzed off and stormed out. I'd never seen her that angry before ... except for maybe one time by the lake a couple of summers ago. When Jackie Chapman scratched her new Walkman. It was a proper Sony and everything. A red one. Jackie dropped it on the rocks so it got scratched and dented. Zoe didn't talk to her after that. At least, not until the lights came. Then everything changed.

NIGHT HOUSE AGENT: When did you next see Zoe?

TARA FISHER: Monday morning. She always met me outside my house. Then we'd walk to Dennis's, then the three of us walked to school.

NIGHT HOUSE AGENT: That would be Monday, 26th November. And how did Zoe seem?

TARA FISHER: Weird. Or different anyway. Like, she hardly said a word. And when she did, she was like a robot, you know? No expression. And then she did this weird thing on the crossing near school. The lights went red, so all the cars stopped and we went over, but when we were halfway across, Zoe stopped. Right in the middle of the road. And she wouldn't move. The lights went green, and the cars wanted to go, but Zoe just stood there. She was, like, staring. Eyes wide open. And she was mumbling something. Me and Dennis didn't know what to do at first. Then I sort of grabbed her arm and shook her, and she looked at me and growled. Actually growled. Like ... *grrrr*. And it was scary cos I could tell she wasn't joking. She was sort of ... like an animal. Anyway, a man got out of his car and started shouting at us, and that's when Zoe blinked and it was like she was

Zoe again instead of ... I dunno ... whatever she was just before that. She looked at us all confused and said, "What's wrong with me?" then she zoned out again and just walked off as if nothing had happened.

NIGHT HOUSE AGENT: You said she was mumbling. Do you remember what she was saying?

TARA FISHER: Yeah, I do. She was saying the numbers.

Tuesday, 27th November 1984

Tara Fisher was kneeling on the sofa and looking out of the front window of the flat she lived in with her mum. The flat was above her mum's antiques shop in the not-so-nice part of Wintermoor. It was early morning and still dark outside. Snow had fallen during the night, and a thin layer of white covered the grey pavement.

Every time Tara saw a figure approaching, she leaned close to the glass, hoping it was Zoe. But it never was.

"You'll just have to go without her," Tara's mum said, snatching her keys from the table. "You'll be late for school. Come on."

Tara shivered and shuffled off the sofa. She wanted to tell her mum she was worried about Zoe. She thought something might be wrong with her since she'd told Tara and the others about the light in the sky. But when Tara tried to figure out how to say it, it felt so silly that she didn't say anything.

Instead, she grabbed her school bag and followed her mum downstairs to the small hallway by the front door. That's where they hung their coats and stored a few things they didn't want to take upstairs, like the old bike that Tara's mum wheeled out every morning to lean by the shop door. It was black and spotted with patches of brown rust, with a basket on the front. The word "Antiques" was painted in white on a piece of wood tied to the basket. Mum said it added an "authentic feel" to the shop. The bike probably wasn't worth anything, but they always brought it into the flat at night so it didn't get stolen.

Tara took her coat and opened the front door. She waited for her mum to wheel the bicycle outside, then she closed the door behind her.

"Have a good day," Tara's mum said. "Work hard." Then she headed along the pavement to lean the bicycle against the wall and open the shop that never had any customers.

Tara walked in the opposite direction. The thin layer of snow softened her footsteps and dulled the world. She took the side streets and alleys, passing the big houses. When she turned onto Becker Street, she saw her friend Dennis waiting outside his house. He was wearing the long black coat he had bought for five quid in the Oxfam shop on the high street. Dennis called it his "grandad coat". His scruffy black hair stuck out in all directions, and he was wearing fingerless woollen gloves. The gloves were soaking wet because he was compacting a snowball with both hands.

"You're late," he said when he saw Tara. "Where's Zoe?"

"Dunno." Tara shrugged. "She didn't show."

"D'you think she's all right?" Dennis chucked the snowball across the road. It hit a wall and exploded like a hand grenade.

"She's been acting weird," Tara replied. "And I've got a bad feeling. Like something's wrong, you know?"

"Yeah." Dennis sniffed and picked up his canvas school bag. It had been lying in the snow like a dead animal. "I know what you mean."

As they set off, Tara looked back, hoping to see Zoe running to catch up with them, but there was no sign of her.

—

When Tara and Dennis arrived at school, the corridor in the new block was crazy busy. There were kids everywhere, and all the windows were dripping with condensation.

Tara and Dennis pushed through the crowd towards their classroom. Miss James wasn't there yet, so the noise level was high. Everyone was talking at once, getting louder and louder. Some boys were kicking a ball of scrunched-up paper backwards and forwards in front of Miss James's desk.

Tara stopped dead as soon as she walked in.

"Look," she said to Dennis. "Zoe's already here."

"What?" Dennis pushed into the room beside her.

"Over there." Tara tilted her head towards the back of the class where Zoe was sitting at a table that was normally spare. In the seat beside her was Jackie Chapman – her *arch-enemy*. Except the two of them didn't look like enemies right now. They were huddled together, deep in conversation.

Jackie's place at her usual table was empty, and her best friend, Helen Pike, was in the chair beside it. Helen was dramatically flicking her ponytail and glaring at Jackie and Zoe.

"What the hell?" Dennis said. "Zoe hates Jackie after that thing with her Walkman and—"

"Zoe blanked me," Jasmine said, coming over. "What's going on?"

Jasmine Russell was the fourth member of Tara's friendship group. It had always been the four of them. Zoe, Dennis, Jasmine and Tara. They had been best friends since Infants. But Zoe and Tara had always been the closest.

Jasmine was wearing a leather biker jacket over her uniform, and her hair was back-combed, even though both of those things were against school rules. She was chewing bubble gum, which was also highly illegal at Wintermoor Comprehensive. Miss James would tell her to take the jacket off and lose the gum as soon as she saw her.

"They've been sitting like that since I got here," Jasmine told them. "I tried to talk to Zoe, but she didn't even look at me. Is there something I don't know about?"

Tara shook her head. She could feel herself getting angry. She had been friends with Zoe for *ever*. They did everything together, told each other everything.

Before she could stop herself, Tara threw her bag on the table she always sat at with Zoe and marched over to where Zoe and Jackie were huddled.

"I waited for you," Tara said, putting her hands on her hips and frowning at Zoe. "I waited *ages*."

Zoe stopped mid-sentence but didn't move. She stayed exactly as she was, face close to Jackie's, the two of them staring directly into each other's eyes.

"Excuse me," Tara said sarcastically. "Did you hear what I said?"

When Zoe finally turned and looked up, there was something dark and mean in her eyes.

"Do you mind?" Zoe said in a flat tone. "This is a private conversation."

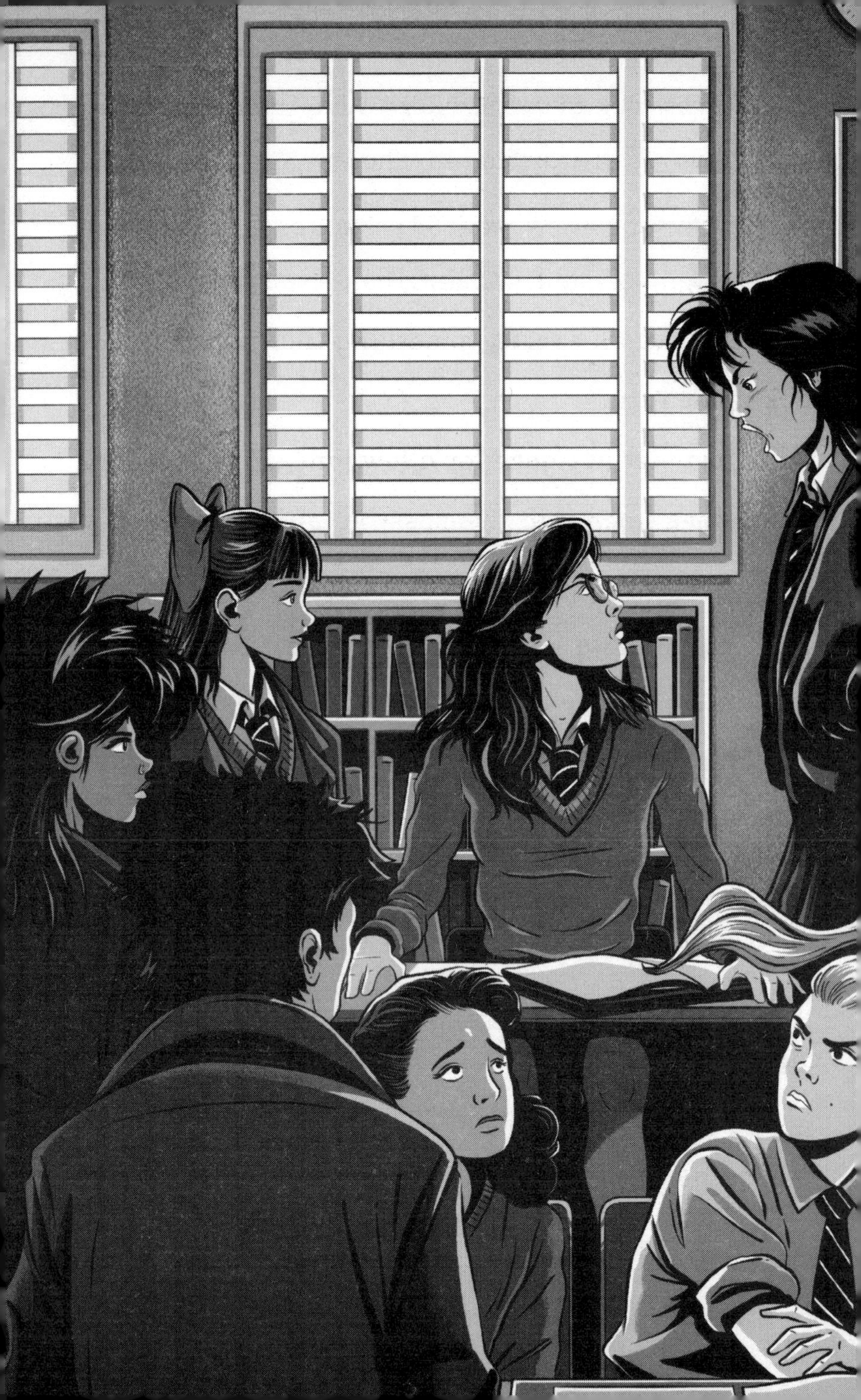

"What? I ... well, I won't wait for so long tomorrow," Tara stammered. She knew it was a weak comeback, and she felt embarrassed for herself.

"Fine," Zoe said. "Don't." Then she leaned closer to Jackie and whispered something that made Jackie look up at Tara.

Tara met her gaze for a few long seconds before Miss James came into the classroom, clapped her hands and shouted, "Seats, everyone!"

Tara went to her usual place, feeling angry and confused. Dennis and Jasmine sat together while she sat alone at the table for the first two lessons of the morning. From time to time, she looked back at Zoe and Jackie, who sat up straight, facing the front as if they were perfect students.

At the end of the lesson, Dennis and Jasmine came over while Tara was still packing up her books.

"What's up with them?" Dennis said.

"Who cares?" Tara replied, trying to pretend she wasn't hurt.

"Hey," Dennis called to Helen, who was on her way out of the classroom.

Helen stopped in the doorway.

"What do *you* want, freak?" she said.

Dennis ignored the insult. "What's up with Jackie? When did she and Zoe start hanging out?"

Helen shrugged. "Who cares? I haven't spoken to Jackie since yesterday. I think she's annoyed or something."

"About what?" Dennis asked.

Helen chewed the inside of her cheek, trying to decide whether or not to tell.

"Come on," Dennis persisted. "Spill it."

Helen rolled her eyes. "It's no big deal. She told me some stupid story about lights, and I thought she was winding me up, and now she won't talk to me."

"Lights?" Tara asked. "What kind of lights? What story?"

"She told me she saw a light in the sky," Helen said. "That it came down and then disappeared. I did an *E.T. Phone Home* joke, and now she won't talk to me."

Tara, Dennis and Jasmine looked at each other, all of them making the connection at the same time. Zoe had told *them* a story about seeing a light too.

"Let's go and find Zoe," Dennis said. "Find out what's going on."

They spent the whole of break-time looking for Zoe but couldn't find her anywhere. And the same thing happened at lunch-time – Zoe seemed to just disappear. In fact, the only time Tara saw Zoe that day was during lessons. And when Tara tried to talk to her, Zoe blanked her.

Tara was in a foul mood when she got home. Her mum asked what was wrong, but Tara was too upset to even talk about it. She told her mum she had homework and shut herself in her room to listen to some music.

On Wednesday morning, it was snowing again. Tara watched from the window in the living room, waiting for Zoe, but not for as long as she had waited on Tuesday. When Zoe didn't turn up, Tara walked alone to meet Dennis, and the two of them went to school without her.

Once again, she didn't see Zoe all day except for in class.

On Thursday morning, Tara didn't bother waiting even for a minute. She put on her coat and trainers and went straight out onto the snowy streets of Wintermoor. She walked to Dennis's house and then to school, knowing that Zoe would already be there, sitting at the back of the class with Jackie.

But then something happened at lunch-time.

Something that terrified Tara.

Thursday, 29th November 1984

Tara was in the busy dining hall, finishing a bag of Quavers. Her cheese sandwich was lying half eaten in her lunchbox. The hall echoed with kids' chatter, and the stale air smelled of boiled cabbage and old chip oil.

"Is it me?" Tara asked Jasmine, who was sitting opposite her. "Did I do something to annoy Zoe?"

"Nope." Jasmine pinched a thick strand of bubble gum and stretched it from between her teeth. "She's the same with me and Dennis." She pushed the gum back into her mouth and pointed towards the door. "Speak of the Devil …"

Tara looked over her shoulder to see Dennis standing in the doorway. He was wearing his coat, as usual, and had a guitar case slung over his shoulder. Dennis spotted Tara and Jasmine and began picking his way among the busy tables towards them.

"Hey," he said, swinging a leg over the bench and sitting down. "Guess what I just saw."

"I don't know." Tara shrugged. "What?"

"Guess," Dennis insisted.

"We literally have no idea." Jasmine rolled her eyes. "Just tell us."

"Well," Dennis said, drawing it out, "I was coming out of my guitar lesson, and I saw Zoe."

Tara was confused. "OK. So what?"

"*So* ..." Dennis paused for dramatic effect. "I know where she's been going at break-time."

Tara was suddenly intrigued. She glanced at Jasmine, whose expression had changed from boredom to interest.

"Go on then." Jasmine leaned forwards. "Where?"

Dennis shrugged. "I'll show you."

The music building where Dennis had his guitar lessons was at the far corner of the school playground. It was tall and narrow and wonky, and must have been at least two hundred years old. It looked as if it might fall down at any moment. Icicles hung from the guttering like dangerous teeth.

Tara and Jasmine followed Dennis across the playground, dodging a massive Fourth Form snowball fight. Kids were running everywhere, pelting snowballs in all directions.

"Jeez." Dennis swore as one whizzed past his nose. "Watch it!"

They kept their heads down and made it to the music building. Tara was half expecting Dennis to lead them inside, but he took them round the back, where there was a narrow alley between the building and the wall that surrounded the playground. The snow there was a mosaic of footprints leading to a rickety wooden door set into the wall.

"Here?" Tara asked when Dennis stopped by the door. "The Walled Garden?"

The Walled Garden had been out of bounds for as long as Tara and her friends had been at Wintermoor Comprehensive School. Years ago, it had been a place for kids to learn about growing plants and keeping small animals. There had been a chicken run, a hutch with a few rabbits, that kind of thing. Now, though, it was off-limits. The land was going to be used to extend the school – eventually.

"Yep," Dennis said in a matter-of-fact way. "This is where they went." He pointed at the broken lock, then gave the rickety door a push to prove that it was open.

"Want to go in?" he grinned.

"God, yes." Jasmine looked eager. "I've never been in there before."

"Me neither. I've only ever seen it from up

there." Dennis looked up at the top window of the music building.

"Same," Tara said. "But ... are you sure? We're not supposed to go in there. It's out of bounds."

"That didn't stop *them*," Dennis said. "Come on." He pushed the door wider.

The rusty hinges didn't squeak as Tara might have expected. Instead, the gate opened smoothly until it pushed against something spongy and wouldn't open any further. Dennis edged sideways through the opening.

Jasmine followed, then Tara.

———

It was a jungle of brambles that blocked the gate from opening properly, their thick stems bristling with savage thorns. But someone had cut a path through them, and footprints led along it. There was just enough room for Tara and her friends to follow the path without scratching themselves, then they were on a stone patio with steps leading down to the main garden.

The footprints continued down the steps, across the long grass and disappeared behind an area of dense shrubs. Somewhere beyond that, Tara could make out the roof of a large, ramshackle shed in the far corner of the garden.

"Shall we?" Dennis gestured at the footprints.

Tara pulled her coat tight against the cold. She had a strange feeling churning in her stomach. She didn't know if it was because she felt guilty about spying on Zoe or because she thought something bad was about to happen.

She took a deep breath and nodded. "OK."

In single file, they followed the footprints down the steps and around the shrubs, then paused. They could now see what had once been a chicken run, close to the old shed. It was an area about the size of Tara's kitchen, surrounded by a rotten fence and rusted chicken wire.

A group of kids was standing inside it.

One of those kids was Zoe. She was unmistakable with her bright red coat and her long auburn hair. Jackie was there also, as well as two boys without coats.

"That's Connor Benchley," Jasmine whispered. "And ... Jack Martin, I think."

The four kids were standing in a circle inside the chicken run, facing each other. They were completely upright, backs straight. Their breath was puffing out in the cold, and their lips were moving as if they were all talking at the same time. Tara could hear the sound of their voices but not what they were saying.

"So creepy." Dennis shivered. "Are they chanting?"

"It's like they're praying or something," Jasmine said. "Weird. They're ... wait. Who's that?"

To their left, a figure stepped out from behind a trellis that was thick with snow-covered ivy. Tara and the others hadn't realised they weren't the only

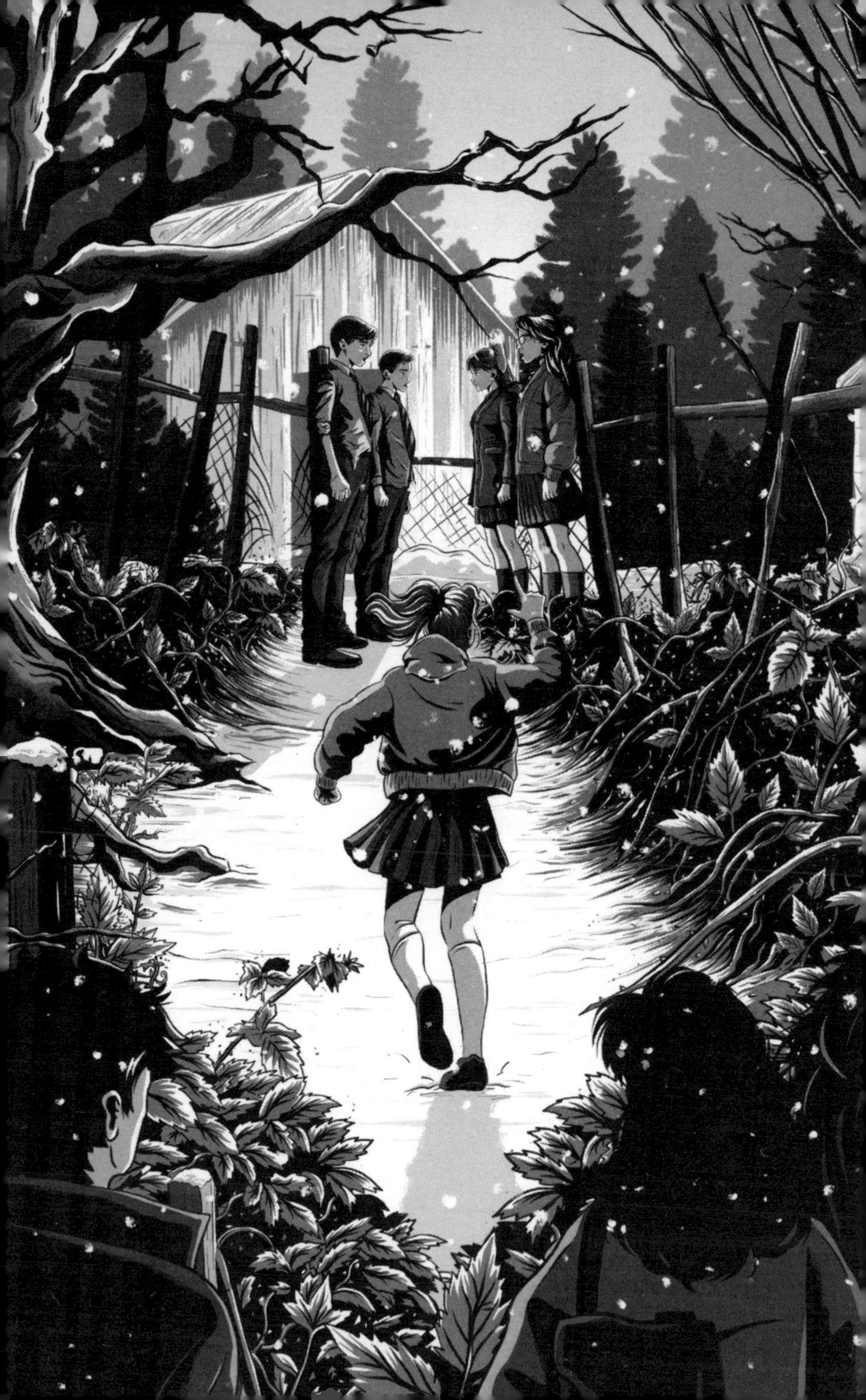

ones watching the bizarre behaviour inside the chicken run. Helen, Jackie's former best friend, must have sneaked into the garden earlier to find out what was going on and had now decided to reveal herself.

Helen marched across the garden towards the group, her ponytail bouncing on her shoulders. At first, it seemed as if Zoe and the others hadn't noticed her, but when Helen stepped through a gap in the fence around the chicken run, they moved closer together.

Tara could hear Helen saying something to them. She was waving her hands about, clearly upset, but Jackie ignored her. However, when Helen put her hand on Jackie's shoulder, the situation suddenly took a dangerous turn.

Jackie growled like a wild animal and shoved Helen with such force that she fell backwards. There was a hollow thump as her head hit the frozen earth, then she lay still.

Zoe and the two boys came to Jackie's side, the

four of them forming a semicircle around Helen, who was lying motionless on the ground. Then Jackie stooped to pick up a broken fence post. She inspected the nasty, jagged point at one end, then stepped closer to stand directly over Helen. Jackie raised the broken fence post with both hands, as if she was about to drive it downwards.

Tara was both terrified and fascinated by what she was seeing. She knew that Jackie was about to hurt Helen – and hurt her *badly*. She also knew she had to stop it, but she didn't know how.

It was Dennis who acted first.

"Hey!" he shouted. "Leave her alone!"

Zoe and the others jerked their heads around to look over at him. They stared for a moment, then Jackie dropped the broken fence post and started walking quickly towards them, closely followed by Zoe and the two boys.

They acted together, like robots. As if they were silently communicating with each other. And they came *so* fast, Tara thought they were going to walk right into her. But at the last moment, Zoe and the others turned just enough to brush past Tara and her friends.

They stomped up the patio steps.

"What's going on?" Tara called after Zoe. "What are you all doing?"

But they didn't stop. They pushed through the brambles and out of the garden.

Friday, 30th November 1984

On Friday, things got worse.

After school, Tara went with Dennis and Jasmine to the Roxy Cinema on the high street to see *The Karate Kid*. The film had come out a few months earlier, but the Roxy was small and always showed films ages after everywhere else.

Tara hadn't felt like going because she was still angry about what had happened in the Walled Garden. But Dennis kept pestering her, saying she needed a distraction, so she finally agreed to go. Also, the Roxy had Butterkist toffee popcorn, which was her favourite.

When the film ended, everyone bustled out into the cold evening.

"D'you reckon I could learn karate like that?" Dennis said as they turned off the high street and started making their way up Dobson Road, the steepest street in Wintermoor. "Wax on. Wax off." He circled his arms as if he was blocking punches. "I reckon I could."

Dobson Road was quiet, with cosy lights glowing behind closed curtains on all the houses that faced the pavement.

"Of course not," Tara told him. "It's a film. It's made up."

"My cousin does karate," Jasmine offered. "He's been doing it for two years, and I can still beat him in a fight."

"Isn't he, like, six years old or something?" Dennis asked. He stood on one leg and spread out his arms like the kid at the end of the film but quickly lost his balance and almost fell over.

"He's seven." Jasmine blew a bubble with her gum and popped it. "And he's a pain in the bum."

"I wish Zoe had come," Tara said. "She would've liked it."

They were close to the top of Dobson Road, a place that gave one of the best views over Wintermoor.

"I did *call* her," Dennis said. "But Zoe wouldn't even come to the phone. Her mum said she wasn't feeling well."

"What's going on with her?" Tara asked. "Why won't she talk to us? And why is she hanging out with Jackie and them?"

"Who cares?" Dennis said. "If she wants to be like that, let her. It's like they're in a cult or something."

"I don't get it," Tara argued. "Why is she—"

"Hey, guys. *Guys*," Jasmine said. "Look at that."

Tara and Dennis hadn't noticed that Jasmine had stopped walking with them. When they turned around, they saw that she was standing still, staring through the gap between two big houses.

Tara felt her stomach tighten. "Look at what?" she asked, not wanting to know the answer.

"There." Jasmine pointed between the houses. "There's a light. Above the woods."

"Oh jeez, not you too," Dennis moaned.

"For real," Jasmine said. "Just look. Right there."

Full of dread, Tara walked with Dennis back to where Jasmine was standing. They were at the highest point of Dobson Road. Through the gap between the two big houses, they could see Wintermoor stretching out in front of them, and the darkness of the woods in the distance. The sky was clear, with a glowing fingernail of moon.

"You're just seeing stars," Dennis told her.

"No," Jasmine insisted. "Lower down, over the woods. There's two of them."

Tara strained to see something. Anything.

"How can you not see them?" Jasmine sounded

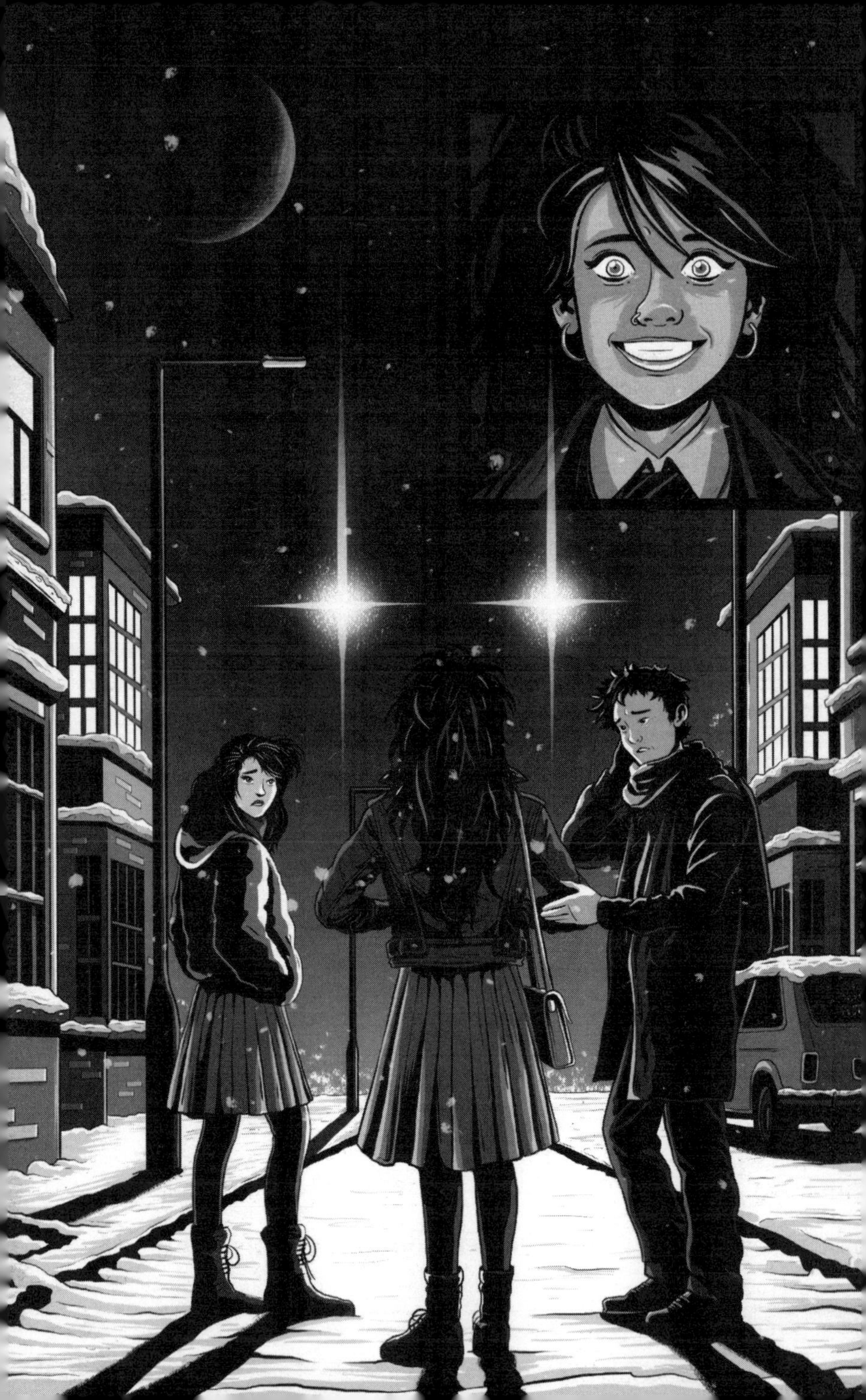

annoyed. "They're right *there*. Moving about. Changing colour. They look amazing."

Tara and Dennis shared a glance, then Dennis rolled his eyes and said, "Yeah, yeah, good joke. Come on – let's go. I'm getting cold."

"Amazing," Jasmine said again, staying where she was. Her mouth spread into a too-big smile that creeped Tara out. "They're coming closer."

"You've made your point." Dennis grabbed Jasmine's sleeve. "Let's go."

In that instant, Jasmine's smile dropped away. She turned on Dennis, eyes flashing with violent anger.

"Get off me!" she growled, pulling away from him.

"Whoa." Dennis held up his hands. "I'm sorry, OK?"

But Jasmine ignored him. Her too-big smile returned, and she looked back at the sky. Staring.

"They're coming closer," Jasmine said, tilting

her head back so she could look straight up. "One of them has stopped right above me. It's *right there*. Can't you see it?"

"Wait ..." Tara whispered. "I think I *do* see something. Is that ...?"

There was some kind of glow above Jasmine. And maybe – *maybe* – it was coming lower, but ... then it was gone.

"No. Sorry," Tara said. "I just thought—" She stopped when she saw that Jasmine was standing rigid, arms by her sides, facing forwards. She looked as if she had been frozen on the spot.

Turned to stone.

That's when Tara noticed someone on the pavement on the other side of the road. A kid with his back to her and his hood up so she couldn't see his face. He was on his own, standing dead still like a statue. Just like Jasmine.

Tara nudged Dennis and pointed.

"That's freaky," she said.

"What the hell?" Dennis peered across the road. "Who *is* that? Is this some kind of joke?"

"I don't like it," Tara whispered.

"All right, you can stop now," Dennis said, turning to Jasmine and waving a hand in front of her face. "You've had your joke. You can stop now. You're scaring us."

Then Jasmine blinked. She looked at Dennis and said something that would haunt Tara for the rest of her life.

"It's waking up," she said. "I am chosen."

REPORT: X5N846-2

CLASSIFIED

TOP SECRET

Interview with: Tara Fisher
Date: Friday, 9th January 1987

The following is taken from an interview with Tara Fisher that took place two years after the incident at Wintermoor.

TARA FISHER: That's exactly what she said. "It's waking up. I am chosen." And the way she said it was like ... she was like a robot or something. No emotion. Totally freaked me out.

NIGHT HOUSE AGENT: Do you know what she meant by it?

TARA FISHER: No. I mean, I do now, but I didn't then.

NIGHT HOUSE AGENT: Can you tell me what happened next?

TARA FISHER: Well, then she just sort of snapped out of it. She even asked us where the lights had gone. And I saw the kid on the other side of the road looking about like he'd forgotten where he was. I realised who it was then. It was Peter Nolan from school. He saw us but didn't say anything. He just walked off. Going home or whatever. Jasmine did the same, and it gave me the creeps.

NIGHT HOUSE AGENT: But *you* think you saw a light? The same light Jasmine saw?

TARA FISHER: I saw *something*. It was faint. Not like what Jasmine said, but definitely *something*. I think maybe she was the only one who was supposed to see it, you know? Or maybe

Peter Nolan saw it too. The kid who was on the other side of the road that night.

NIGHT HOUSE AGENT: I'm not sure I understand what you mean.

TARA FISHER: Well, Jasmine said there were two lights, didn't she? But only one stopped above her. So maybe the second light went to Peter. He is one of the kids who said they saw a light. So maybe that's when he saw it. And I'm thinking that maybe Jasmine and Peter were the only ones who saw the lights properly that night cos they were the ones who were supposed to see them. Does that make sense? Anyway, they both changed. The lights changed them.

NIGHT HOUSE AGENT: In what way?

TARA FISHER: Jasmine started hanging out with Zoe and Jackie after that. Wouldn't talk to me and Dennis any more. We went upstairs in the music building at break-times and watched them in the garden. Not just Jasmine and Zoe, but other kids from my year too. Ones who said they'd seen lights. Including Peter Nolan. They stood there in a circle, talking all at the same time. And we weren't the only ones to notice. Other kids said their friends were acting weird – said they'd seen them standing in the street at night, staring at the sky. And there were more kids in the garden every day. Even Helen – Jackie's friend who got pushed over that time? Even she joined them. It got so there were, like, ten of them. Dennis said it was a cult, like that weird cult where the guy made them all drink poison. And that got me really scared because I didn't know what they were going to do. I told my mum cos you're supposed to tell an adult, but she just said it was probably a prank. It wasn't, though, cos then something happened that really scared me. I thought I was going to die.

Excerpt from TARA FISHER'S DIARY

Wednesday, 5th December 1984

Worst day ever. Something happened in PE, and I can't stop thinking about it. I didn't even have Dennis there to stick up for me. I've never felt so horrible and lonely before. We were playing netball, which is already my worst thing to do in PE.

Zoe and Jackie were on the same team with some of the kids who are acting weird - like Helen Pike and Lisa Canning. I was on the other team, playing goal shooter, and Zoe blocked me from scoring. But she was really mean when she did it. She was staring right at me, and she got really close and pushed me really hard. And I suddenly got angry. I couldn't help it. It's like everything just boiled up inside me, and I pushed her back and told her to stop being such a B-word.

Miss Young blew her whistle and told me off in front of everyone, and I was so embarrassed.

Everyone was looking at me. All the kids. Then Miss Young told me to sit at the side, but when I started walking away, Zoe pushed me hard in the back, and I went flying. I've got scrapes all over my knees from where I skidded on the floor. There's also a bad one on my elbow. It's all red raw like a carpet burn, and it really hurts.

At first, I was confused because it took me by surprise, and I didn't know what had happened. Then I tried to get up, but someone kicked my arm and I fell flat on my face. My nose banged into the floor, and my eyes were watering. I was trying not to cry, but I was so scared, especially when I turned over and saw Zoe, Jasmine, Jackie and Ayesha standing around me, looking down.

Miss Young was blowing her whistle and shouting at them, but they just ignored her. Then Zoe stood on my fingers. <u>Really hard</u>. She was wearing her trainers with the chunky grips, and she pressed down so hard it made me scream. She even twisted her foot to make it hurt extra. I thought something was broken!

Then she suddenly stopped, like someone flicked a switch. She moved her foot and stood there with Jasmine and Jackie and Ayesha just looking down at me. Then they started speaking. All of them at the same time, saying the same thing. It was numbers. They were saying numbers. But that wasn't the worst thing. The worst thing was what they looked like. Their faces were all blurred. At first, I thought it was because I was crying, but when I wiped my eyes, it was the same. Their faces were gone.

REPORT: X5N846-3

CLASSIFIED

TOP SECRET

Interview with: Tara Fisher
Date: Friday, 9th January 1987

The following is taken from an interview with Tara Fisher that took place two years after the incident at Wintermoor.

NIGHT HOUSE AGENT: In your diary entry from Wednesday, 5th December, you wrote that your friends' faces were "gone". What did you mean by that?

TARA FISHER: I dunno. It's like ... like they were blurry. Like I couldn't see their eyes or nose or mouth or anything. Just a blur of light and colours. It was horrible.

NIGHT HOUSE AGENT: And you mentioned that they were reciting numbers.

TARA FISHER: Yeah. All saying the same numbers at the same time. Like they'd practised it.

NIGHT HOUSE AGENT: Did the numbers mean anything to you?

TARA FISHER: No. Not then. It was much later when I found out what the numbers meant.

Friday, 7th December 1984

It was the first lesson of the day, and Tara was struggling to concentrate. The scrapes on her knees were throbbing, and every time she leaned on her desk, the graze on her elbow stung like her whole arm was on fire.

But there was something else bothering Tara.

Zoe, Jasmine, Jackie and Helen weren't in class that morning. The teacher had asked if anyone knew where they were, but Tara didn't have a clue. She pretended she didn't care after what had happened during PE on Wednesday. But she *did* care. Deep down, she was worried about Zoe and Jasmine despite everything that had happened.

So Tara slumped in the seat beside Dennis while Mr Gregory wrote on the board and droned on about ratios.

That was when Tara noticed the graffiti.

It looked fresh and was scratched into the top-left corner of the desk. Someone must have used the sharp point of a compass to do it, then written over it with black ink to make it stand out.

It said: *It's waking up.*

The sight of it was like an electric shock. Tara jerked back as if the words were dangerous. She elbowed Dennis in the arm.

"Did you see this?" She pointed at the graffiti. "It's what Jasmine said that night."

"Yeah." Dennis glanced up to check Mr Gregory hadn't heard them. "There's this too." He showed her more writing scratched into the top-right corner of the desk.

This one said: *I am chosen*.

"You think it was her?" Tara asked.

"Nah. It's on the wall in the boys' toilets too."

"What?" Tara asked.

"That exact thing is on the wall in the boys' toilets," Dennis said. "And it's scratched on one of the lockers in the changing rooms. I think—"

"Do you have something you want to share with the rest of the class, David Takagi?" Mr Gregory interrupted, making him and Tara look up in alarm.

"Err ... No, sir," Dennis said.

Mr Gregory sighed. "So you won't mind if we get on with the lesson then?"

"No, sir," Dennis said. "I'd like that very much, sir."

"In which case," said Mr Gregory, "everybody can do the exercises on page thirty-seven. In silence. Courtesy of Mr Takagi."

There was a quiet groan from the class but less than normal. Usually, there would have been a few giggles, maybe even Mr Gregory might have smiled. But not that day. Because everything was different now. There was a weird atmosphere around school, and something wasn't quite right. Tara was sure that the other kids felt it, and she thought the teachers felt it too.

She glanced over her shoulder at the empty seats at the back of the class and wondered where Zoe, Jasmine, Helen and Jackie might be.

At break-time, there was still no sign of Tara's missing friends, and it turned out they weren't the only ones who were absent from school. Tara started to hear about other kids who hadn't come in that morning. In fact, everyone was talking about it, and the rumours were getting worse. At first, people were saying three other kids were missing, then it was five, then ten, but nobody really knew for sure. Tara and Dennis sneaked into the music building and went to the room at the top to look into the Walled Garden, hoping they might see something. The snow was trampled from where the kids had been in there the day before, but the only thing visible now was a solitary magpie hopping about on the shed roof.

Tara couldn't help feeling worried, despite being angry with Zoe and Jasmine. She didn't want anything bad to happen to them. But she *knew* something bad had happened when she saw the police car. She was in the Art room, not long before lunch, when she glanced out of the window and saw it pulling into the school car park. Two police officers climbed out and trudged across the snow towards reception.

A few minutes later, the school secretary, Mrs Button, knocked on the Art room door.

"Tara?" said Mrs Button. "The headmaster wants to see you in his office."

Excerpt from TARA FISHER'S DIARY

Friday, 7th December 1984

When the secretary called me out of class, I didn't know why. I knew it was something bad though. It had to be. So I started getting all these ideas of things it could be. Like maybe it was something to do with Zoe. Or Jasmine. <u>Or Mum!</u> Everyone was staring at me, and I was suddenly <u>positive</u> something horrible had happened to Mum. Like, she'd been hurt, or there had been a fire in the shop or something. Oh my God, just thinking about it makes me feel sick.

So anyway, the secretary took me straight into Mr McNab's office, and he was there with the policeman and the policewoman. My heart was racing so fast I thought I was going to throw up. They told me to sit down, and they smiled and said they had found Zoe. It wasn't anything to do with Mum, and I was so relieved I didn't hear what the police said next. I had to say "Pardon?" so they started again. They said Zoe was on Reacher's Lane and someone nearly ran her over but didn't. I don't know why she was on Reacher's Lane - it's nowhere near her house. In fact, it's on the way out of town, so why was she there? They found Jasmine too, on the high street, just wandering about in a daze and mumbling to herself like Zoe was. Then the police wanted to know if Zoe or Jasmine had any problems at home or with boyfriends. Or if they'd been in trouble. I don't know about that because I don't even talk to them any more, but I told the police about the garden and the lights and the graffiti I saw on the desk.

I could tell Mr McNab was annoyed because he kind of huffed and shook his head as soon as I mentioned the lights.

"What's all this about lights?" said the policeman, and I'm not going to lie, he looked annoyed too. Worse even than Mr McNab. He had really pale blue eyes, lots of freckles and a bushy moustache. His cheeks were all red from the cold outside, and he looked a bit like he might explode.

He said, "Is there some kind of joke going on? You need to tell us the truth because we won't tolerate children wasting our time," or something like that.

Straight away I didn't like him.

"I've seen something," I told him. "When Jasmine said she saw lights, I saw something too. In the sky above her, and then it disappeared."

I could tell no one believed me, but why would I make it up? It was so annoying. Why does no one ever listen to what kids tell them? I wasn't making it up, and I said so, but the policeman kept talking right over me and telling me not to be so silly. SO ANNOYING!

I couldn't think straight, but then I thought I knew how to make them listen.

"Was she saying numbers?" I asked.

And that made them all stop. Even the policeman looked at me like I'd said something really important.

"What made you ask that?" he said.

"Because I've heard them," I said. "In class. And in the garden."

"What do the numbers mean?" the policewoman asked.

I said I didn't know what the numbers mean. And I told them how I'd seen Zoe and the others go to the garden and stand in a circle, staring at each other, saying the numbers.

Then Mr McNab looked at me really serious and said, "I'm surprised at you, Tara. I would never have expected you to get involved in a silly prank like this."

I tried to tell them it wasn't a stupid prank, but they wouldn't listen. A prank? They think it's a prank? Ugh. I hate that word. Even Dennis has started to say it's a stupid "prank" now, but it isn't. I just know it. I think it's been going on for too long. And Zoe is different now. Like she's not really Zoe any more, and it scares me.

Saturday, 8th December 1984

Tara got up early that Saturday. Usually, she loved her lie-in and could stay in bed for hours drifting in and out of sleep – but not that morning. She woke at seven, her head muddled with thoughts of kids missing from school, lights in the sky and strange graffiti.

When she went into the kitchen, her mum was sitting at the little table. She was sipping her tea and reading the local newspaper.

"You're early," she said, making a point of checking the clock on the wall. "What's the occasion?"

Tara ignored her and flicked on the kettle to make a cup of tea.

"There's toast if you want it," Tara's mum said as she went back to reading the newspaper. "And that chocolate spread you like."

"Thanks," Tara mumbled as she reached into the cupboard for her *Knight Rider* mug.

"What is wrong with the children?" Tara's mum asked.

Tara froze with her hand still in the cupboard. "What?"

"That's what it says here." Her mum tapped the newspaper, then began reading aloud. "On Friday this week, a dozen children failed to turn up for lessons at Wintermoor Comprehensive ..." She stopped and took off her glasses. "Did you know about this? Why didn't you say anything?"

Tara carefully put her mug on the worktop.

"What's it all about?" Her mum sounded concerned. "Do you know any of the children who were missing?"

Tara nodded and felt a sudden rush of emotions

rising inside her. Tears sprang into her eyes, but that just made her angry because she didn't want to cry.

She snatched up the box of teabags from beside the kettle.

"They're not missing," Tara said, taking a teabag and throwing it into her mug. "They found them."

"Who was it?" her mum asked.

"Zoe," Tara said. "And Jasmine. And some others."

"Your *friend* Zoe? That's not like her. I hope you're not involved in this. They're saying it's some kind of prank that—"

"I'm *not* involved in it!" Tara turned on her. All her emotions were coming to the surface, just like they had the day Zoe attacked her in netball. "And it's not a prank. There's something wrong with them. I already told you they've been acting weird ever since they saw those lights and—"

"Lights? Isn't that part of the prank?"

"Ugh!" Tara pushed her mug away and stormed

out of the kitchen and down the stairs into the hallway. "No one ever listens to kids, do they? I'm not making it up. I'm not involved. And it's not a prank. It's real!"

"Darling." Her mum went after her. "I'll listen to you. I'll ... wait, where are you going?"

"Out," Tara said, grabbing her coat and shoving her feet into her trainers.

"It's freezing out there," her mum said. "And you haven't had any breakfast."

Tara saw the look on her mum's face and suddenly felt terrible for shouting and getting angry. None of this was her mum's fault. It wasn't fair to get angry with *her*.

"I'm ... I'm sorry," Tara said, deflating. "I just need to get out. I need some space."

Without waiting another moment, she let herself out the front door and headed into the cold.

Tara pulled her coat tight, put her head down and walked quickly along the snowy pavement. She couldn't stop thinking about everything that had happened and how no one believed her when she told them. She wondered if the other kids at school who hadn't seen lights were having the same problem. She knew the police had talked to some of them. Had they said anything? Had they tried to tell their parents? Or maybe they all thought it was some kind of prank too, like Dennis did.

Tara kicked at the snow underfoot, sending a lump of it out into the road. She looked up and saw that she was on Sycamore Road, next to the park. She hadn't planned it, not consciously, but she was on the way to Zoe's house. She realised then that she was going to confront Zoe. She was going to march right up to her front door and demand to know what was going on. She was going to *make* Zoe tell her. So she walked faster, feeling more determined with each step, until she turned onto Zoe's street.

It was a narrow road with wide pavements and enormous, leafless trees that stretched up into the grey sky. Their roots pushed up the paving stones like humpbacked monsters rising from the sea.

Tara headed straight to Zoe's house without pausing. She trudged up the drive and rang the doorbell before she could lose her nerve.

The house was huge. Three storeys high, with a basement and a massive conservatory at the back. It usually took a while before anyone answered the bell.

Tara rang again just as she spotted movement through the frosted glass on the door.

"Yes, can I— Oh, Tara. It's you."

Zoe's mum, who always insisted Tara call her Barbara, was wearing blue jeans and a baggy blazer over a white blouse. Her hair was scrunched in an attempt to look like Madonna. Tara always thought Barbara was a cool mum, but right then she looked tired and worried.

"Is ... is Zoe in?" Tara asked, starting to lose her nerve.

"Oh, Tara darling, come in." Barbara practically dragged Tara into the porch, which was almost as big as Tara's front room.

Beyond the porch was a long hallway, with large doors on the right that opened into the sitting room and the kitchen. At the far end, creaky wooden steps headed down into the back part of the house. To the left, a carpeted staircase led up to the first floor.

"Thank goodness you're here," Barbara continued, running her hands through her hair. "I'm at my wits' end. Maybe you can talk some sense into Zoe. I don't know what's wrong with her. She won't eat, she won't talk, she won't come out of her room ..."

Tara bit her lip and waited for Barbara to stop.

"And then all that fuss about not going to school, and the police and ... she won't talk to me. Do you have any idea what's wrong with her? Is it a boy? Is it a boy, Tara? I could cope with that. And what's all this about lights in the sky and a prank at school?"

"Can I talk to her?" Tara asked, when Barbara finally paused for breath.

"Oh, yes," Barbara said. "Please. I wish you would. Maybe you could—"

"Get rid of her," said a spiteful voice that took them both by surprise.

Tara looked over Barbara's shoulder to see Zoe standing halfway down the carpeted staircase. Her auburn hair was hanging, unbrushed, over her eyes, and her chin was tucked against her chest.

"Get rid of her," Zoe said again, staring directly at Tara. Her voice was pure hatred.

Barbara turned to look at Zoe.

"What's the matter, sweetie?" Barbara asked. "It's Tara. She's come to talk to you. She's your friend."

"No, she isn't," Zoe said. "This is all *her* fault. I wish she'd just leave me alone. Every time I turn around, she's there. Why won't she just leave me alone?"

Barbara turned back to Tara.

"This is *your* fault?" she said. "Did you do something to upset Zoe?"

"No," Tara said, taking a step back. "I haven't done anything."

"Missing school was her idea," Zoe said. "Tara made me do it." She sounded distressed now, almost teary, but she was grinning at Tara. A cold, mean grin beneath cold, dead eyes.

But when Barbara turned to look at Zoe again, Zoe's face dropped into a sad expression.

"It was her idea, Mum," she said. "Honest."

"That's such a lie!" Tara objected. As soon as Barbara turned back to her, Zoe was grinning again. The same sickening grin.

"What's going on?" Tara begged Zoe. "Please tell me."

"I think you'd better just go," Barbara said,

ushering Tara out of the porch. "I don't know why you thought it was a good idea to make Zoe skip school, but I don't want you around her right now."

"I didn't," Tara insisted as she backed out of the front door and onto the step. "She's lying."

"I'm sorry," Barbara said. "Just go."

As Barbara closed the front door, Tara caught a final glimpse of her best friend standing on the staircase, grinning at her. Grinning like a devil.

Tara stood in the cold, watching through the frosted glass door as Zoe's silhouette turned and headed back upstairs while Barbara stood silently in the hallway.

Tara's face burned with embarrassment, and her heart was heavy with betrayal. She couldn't understand why Zoe had lied. Why would she say those things? Why was she being so horrible?

But Tara's visit to Zoe's house was not the most horrible thing to happen to her that day. Because when Tara trudged back down Zoe's drive, she noticed two kids standing under a tree on the other side of the road.

Helen and Peter.

And they were both grinning at her.

Tara watched Helen and Peter, standing beneath the tree, staring at her. Their heads were tilted down slightly, giving them a menacing look. Helen was wearing a yellow coat. Her blonde hair was hanging loose instead of tied back in a ponytail like normal. Peter's bright blue coat was dirty, and he had a red-and-blue bobble hat pulled low over his brow.

"What?" Tara called across the road, challenging them. "What are you looking at?"

Helen and Peter didn't react. They stayed exactly as they were. Motionless. Their mouths remained set in wide and unsettling grins.

Tara scanned the street, but it was deserted.

When she looked back at Helen and Peter, they

were a little closer than before. Not much, but now they were nearer to the kerb.

"Stop it." Tara wrapped her arms around herself and felt a trickle of fear seep through her. "It's not funny. Why are you doing this?"

Helen and Peter took a step forward to the kerb, both at exactly the same time. Right foot then left foot.

"We are chosen," they said as if they had one voice.

"What? What does that even mean?" Tara replied, but the words didn't come out as confidently as she'd intended. Her voice was quiet, and the word "mean" sounded like a squeak.

"We are chosen," they said again, stepping onto the road.

Towards Tara.

"Wh ... whatever," Tara managed to say. She didn't want them to see her fear, so she turned and walked away, striding as confidently as she could.

Her trainers crunched the snow underfoot. The cold stung her ears, and her breath puffed around her.

Tara could feel them watching her. She could feel their dead eyes boring into her back, but she kept walking. Whatever game they were playing, she wasn't going to let them see that they were scaring her. She wouldn't give them the satisfaction. She was going to leave them behind and—

When Tara reached the end of the street and turned onto Richardson Avenue, she risked a quick glance back.

There were three of them now.

Three kids.

Jackie had joined them. She was unmistakable in her pink coat and multicoloured moon boots.

Helen, Peter and Jackie. They were following a few metres behind Tara, completely in step with one another as if they were soldiers marching.

Tara felt like someone had put a cold hand into her chest and wrapped their fingers around

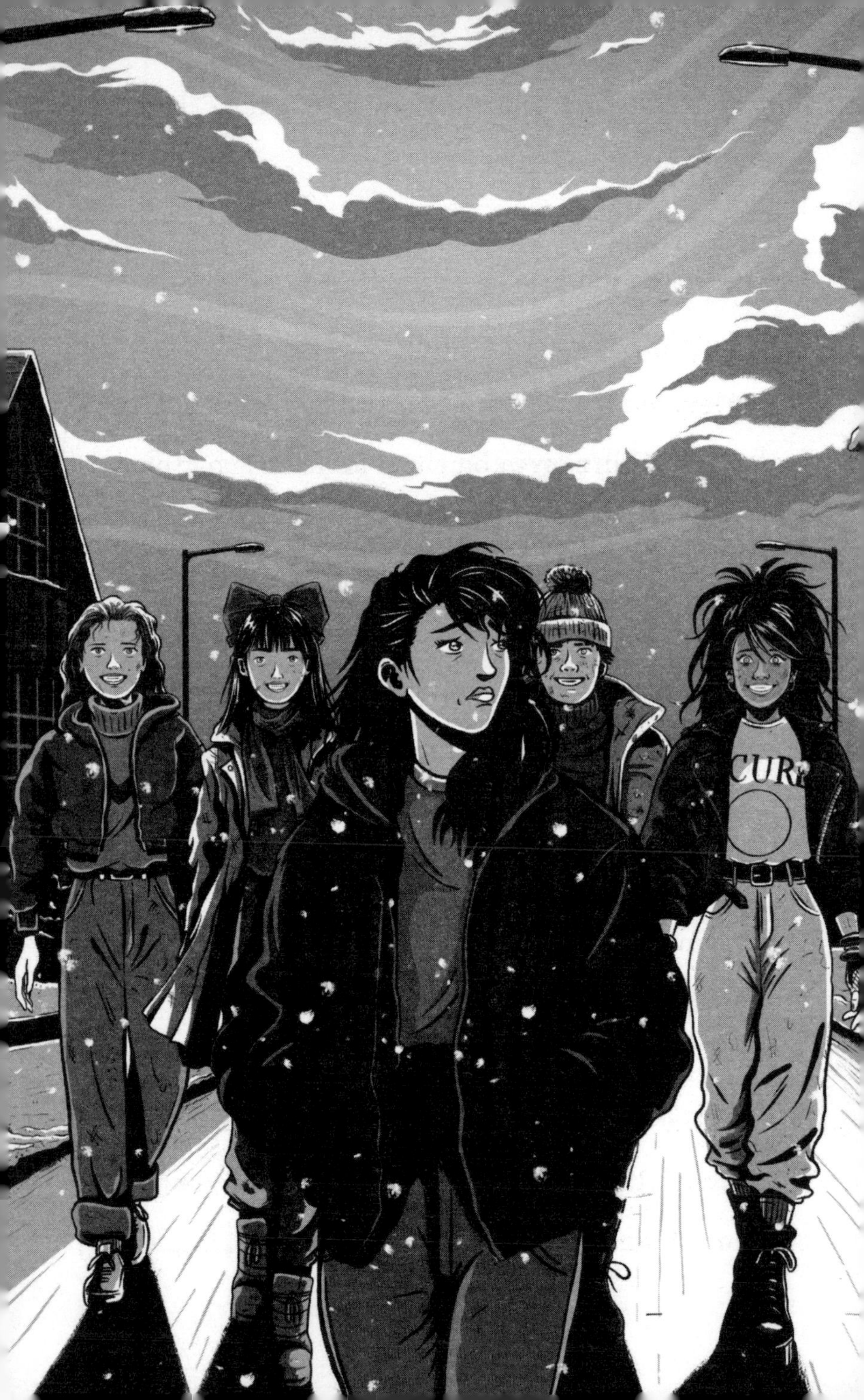

her heart. She felt an awful pressure there, and her stomach tightened.

She picked up her pace, but when she next looked back, there were four of them.

Helen, Peter, Jackie and Jasmine.

They were all walking in time, and they each had that dreadful grin on their face. That awful, wide, ghastly grin.

Tara considered stopping. She thought about confronting them, telling them to leave her alone. But she didn't. She was too afraid. She was terrified of their grins, the deadness of their eyes and the way they were following her. She was convinced they meant to do her harm.

Tara walked as quickly as she could, almost breaking into a run as she reached the end of West Avenue. When she turned the corner, she really *did* start running. She hurried a couple of metres along the street, then ducked down into the alley behind the churchyard. Usually, it was eerie in there, seeing the graves on the other side of the low wall, but Tara didn't even notice them today. There were other, more distressing things to concern her.

She ran to the end of the alley before pausing to check over her shoulder just as the grinning kids entered the alley, still following. Tara didn't wait even a second. She turned left and sprinted along the pavement before she spotted a safe haven on the other side of the road.

The library.

Immediately, she veered across the road towards the large building. She glanced back to check the grinning children hadn't yet emerged from the alley behind the churchyard, then she raced up the library steps and pushed open the door to safety.

—

There was a delicious sense of calm inside the library. The atmosphere was warm and quiet, and the air smelled of dust and paper and polish.

The librarian looked up as Tara entered. She was an older woman, with a rubber stamp in one hand and an open book on the desk in front of her. She wore a floral-patterned blouse, and her greying hair was swept away from her face. She smiled at Tara, then turned her attention back to the book in front of her. She inspected it for damage, placed it on the trolley, then took another book from the pile on her desk.

Tara glanced back through the glass door, making sure the grinning children hadn't seen her, then she headed deeper into the library. Tara was a regular visitor, so she knew where she was going – the far side, close to the picturebook section. There were a couple of tables in the corner that were not visible from the main door. She would be safe there.

But Tara was distracted when she spotted the display of recent newspapers and magazines. The *Saturday Gazette* was there, one of the cover stories screaming at her: "What is wrong with the children?"

It was the same thing her mum had been reading at breakfast.

Tara strode over to the rack, grabbed the newspaper and headed for the safety of the tables at the back of the library. She placed the newspaper flat on a free table, then sat down and read the article three times, feeling all her emotions boiling inside her. Tears gathered in her eyes and welled over. They trickled down her cheekbones and dripped onto the newspaper, where they left large, dark splodges.

"Is everything all right, my dear?"

"Hmm?" Tara looked up and wiped away her tears with the back of her hand.

The librarian was standing in front of Tara's table, both hands grasping the handle of a trolley laden with picturebooks.

"Is everything all right?" she repeated.

"Umm. Yes. I'm fine. Sorry," Tara sniffed.

"No need to apologise," the librarian said

with a sympathetic smile. "It's what we're here for. Somewhere safe to read, to keep warm, to think ... even somewhere to cry, if that's what you need."

Tara didn't reply.

"It's Tara, isn't it?" the librarian asked.

Tara nodded. She had been coming to the library for years, but it was still a surprise that the librarian knew her name.

"You like mysteries and non-fiction if I remember rightly?" the librarian said. "But I've never seen you read the newspaper before." She let go of her trolley and came to stand beside Tara. She looked down at the tear-blotted newspaper. "Are you one of the children who missed school? Did you get into trouble? Is that why you're upset?"

Tara shook her head.

"Then perhaps you know one of them?"

Tara nodded. "Mm-hm."

The librarian pulled out the seat beside Tara's and sat down. She slid the newspaper across the table towards her and read the article. When she was finished, she put her fingers on her chin and looked at Tara.

"I think I might understand how you feel," she said.

Tara frowned.

"Something very similar happened to me," the librarian said. "Or, rather, to a friend of mine."

"Really?" Tara was suddenly interested. "In what way?"

"Well," said the librarian, tapping the newspaper, "it was a long time ago, when I was … oh, I must've been about twelve years old, living on a farm with my parents just outside the village. Wintermoor, I mean. See, it was just a village back then when I was a girl. Not a town. Anyway, during the war, we had children come to the village from all over. They came because it was supposed to be safer here, but …" The librarian sighed. "Well, a girl called Emily came to stay with us on the farm. She was a little older than me, but not much, and we became friends very quickly. Most of the children went back to their homes after just a few months, but Emily's father was killed in the fighting and her mother died in a bombing raid, poor girl, so Emily stayed with us. She became one of the family, really – more like a sister than a best friend. We did everything together. Went to school together, helped out on the farm, fed the animals, and in the summer, we lay in the sun up by the lake. I even taught Emily to swim in that lake."

Tara knew which lake the librarian was talking about. Wintermoor Lake, right in the middle of the woods just outside town. Everyone went up there in the summer. Families took picnics, teenagers found quiet places to hang out, people walked their dogs. It was where Jackie had damaged Zoe's Walkman.

"But then, just out of the blue, Emily started acting strangely," the librarian said. "She started ignoring me and going off on her own all the time.

She didn't want to help out on the farm, or play, or read with me. And sometimes she would just go completely blank, as if – and I know how silly this sounds – but as if she had left her body. And then she started spending time with a boy from the village. A boy called Samuel Kingsley. They were inseparable, and when I tried to talk to her about it, she shut me out. We had been like sisters, and then ... well, then all of a sudden, she didn't want to know me.

"You know, I saw them once, standing face to face, mumbling nonsense at each other for over an hour. Another time, the postman found her wandering about on the road up near the lake as if she had lost her mind. Just like the newspaper says about those children who went missing this week."

"So what happened after that?" Tara's voice came out as a whisper.

The librarian looked at Tara as if she were deciding whether or not to tell her the rest of her story.

"Was it something bad?" Tara asked.

The librarian sighed. "They disappeared. Emily and Samuel. Both on the same day, and not long before Christmas. Someone found a shoe up by the lake, one of Emily's, and people thought she must have fallen in and drowned. Others thought the two of them had run away together, maybe to the city, but those stories didn't make sense to me. Emily could swim – I was the one who taught her – and why would they go to the city? It just didn't feel right."

"So what do you think happened?"

"I have no idea. Not really. But maybe it was something to do with the lights."

The word was like electricity exploding in Tara's chest.

"Lights?" she asked.

"Yes. The article in the newspaper mentions lights. And I remember Emily telling me she had seen a light in the sky. Apparently, Samuel said the same thing."

Tara watched the librarian for a long moment,

wondering whether or not she should ask the question that was burning inside her.

"Were they saying numbers?" she couldn't stop herself asking.

"I beg your pardon?" The librarian's face drained of colour.

"When you saw your friend and that boy facing each other and mumbling nonsense, were they saying numbers?"

"Yes. Yes, they were. But ... how could you possibly know that?"

"Because Zoe was saying numbers," Tara said. "And the others were too. All of them just looking at each other, saying the numbers."

―

"Let me show you something," the librarian said to Tara. "Come with me."

Tara followed her to the back of the library and down a short flight of steps. At the end of a narrow, dark corridor was a door with a stencilled sign on it that read: ARCHIVE. The librarian opened the door and flicked a switch on the wall. A single overhead bulb sparked into life. It illuminated the windowless room with a dull yellow glow.

There were three desks against the back wall of the room. Each had a strange and bulky kind of television standing on it. The walls to either side were lined with metal filing cabinets.

"Have you ever used the microfiche reader before?" the librarian asked.

Tara shook her head.

"Well then," the librarian smiled. "You're about to learn."

She went to one of the filing cabinets and opened a drawer with "Wintermoor Gazette" typed on a label stuck to the front of it. The drawer was filled with boxes, each one about the size and shape of a paperback, stacked sideways. Each box had a year printed on it. The librarian walked two fingers across the boxes until she found the one she was looking for. She took it out of the drawer and briefly held it up for Tara to see.

"1944," she said, carrying it over to one of the desks with a strange television on it.

The librarian put the box on the desk and opened the lid. Inside, there were a number of transparent plastic sheets dotted with tiny dark rectangles.

"These are called microfiches," said the librarian as she flicked through the sheets. "Every microfiche is a piece of film covered with tiny photographs. These ones all have photographs of the *Wintermoor Gazette* on them. And if I remember rightly, one of them will have what I'm looking for on it." She pulled out one of the sheets. "This should be it."

The librarian loaded the rectangular sheet into a tray beneath the strange television machine.

"This is the microfiche reader," she said, pressing a button on the side of the machine. Immediately, the screen lit up and displayed an image of the front cover of the *Wintermoor Gazette*.

"So," said the librarian as Tara watched over her shoulder, "this piece of film features every single newspaper from December 1944, and if I move this, I should be able to find what I'm looking for."

She put her fingers on the tray that she had loaded the film into and slid the tray to one side. The image on the screen blurred as if it was racing though time. When the librarian stopped moving the tray, the image paused, displaying a different edition of the *Wintermoor Gazette*.

"No," the librarian said under her breath before moving the tray once again and navigating to another edition of the newspaper.

"No."

"No."

And so it went on until finally she said, "Here we are."

The date on the front cover now displayed

onscreen was Saturday, 23rd December 1944. The headline was something about the army needing more soldiers, but Tara didn't have time to read it. The librarian scanned away to the other pages of the newspaper until she found something on page ten. It was only a small article, tucked away in the corner as if it was about something unimportant:

> *Police have been searching for missing girl Emily Butcher, aged 14. Emily Butcher was evacuated to Wintermoor in 1940 and has been living at West Lane Farm with Mr and Mrs Creasey and their daughter Irene ever since. The family reported Emily missing on Thursday. Samuel Kingsley, aged 14, a resident of Wintermoor, was also reported missing on the same day. Mr Bernard Kingsley, father of Samuel Kingsley, told the* Wintermoor Gazette *that his son had been acting strangely in*

recent days, following a claim that he had seen a "light in the sky". When asked if he suspected foul play, Police Sergeant Barry Potts told the Wintermoor Gazette: *"I don't think so. I believe the two children have run away and will be found soon enough." The last reported case of a missing person in Wintermoor was that of a young boy in 1904.*

"That's me." The librarian pointed to her name in the article. "Irene Creasey."

Tara nodded, but she was re-reading the article because something had caught her eye. "It says that a boy went missing in 1904," she said quietly.

"Long before my time," Irene replied.

"I wonder what happened to him? Is there any way to find out?"

"Ah, it looks like you have a detective inside you bursting to get out," Irene smiled. "I suppose you could look back and see if there's an article about it. You know how to use the machine now, and the films are all in those filing cabinets. I have to get on, but you're welcome to see what you can find."

The librarian left the microfiche room and closed the door behind her. Tara sat for a second, enjoying the quiet, then she returned the 1944 box to the filing cabinet and began her search.

It didn't take long to find the box containing the 1904 editions of the *Wintermoor Gazette* – except it was called the *Wintermoor and District Gazette* back then. But she had no idea what month she was looking for. Tara decided to begin with the slide labelled January 1904.

Zooming through the slides was exhausting on her eyes and seemed to take for ever. Thankfully, it was a weekly newspaper, so there weren't too many editions. Finally, Tara found what she was looking for. It was only a short article, but it made Tara's blood turn cold.

Constable Bartholomew Jones continues to lead the search for missing boy Bertie Thorne, but hope is fading that he will be found. Bertie disappeared on 10th December after a week of erratic behaviour and claiming to have seen "a strange light in the sky over the lake".

Tara stared at the article for a long time. She read it over and over again, but her eye was drawn to one particular detail. The date at the top of the page.

Saturday, 17th December 1904.

She had a sudden moment of realisation. The date was important. It *meant* something. There was a pattern. But she needed to check through the other old newspapers to be sure.

Tara went to the filing cabinets and looked for a drawer marked 1864. She wondered if there would even *be* newspapers from that long ago. Maybe it was too far back in the past.

But there it was.

1864.

Tara could hardly believe it when she found it. It was the second to last drawer of the very last filing cabinet, right in the corner of the room.

Her heart thumped as she pulled it open and removed the box labelled "1864". Her throat was dry and her fingers trembled as she loaded the slide into the machine. She didn't need to scan through them all. She knew which slide to choose. The one labelled "December".

It wasn't long before Tara found what she was looking for. Again, it was just a small article. No more than a couple of lines.

Eliza Farthing, aged 14, is missing from Wintermoor village. Plagued by peculiar behaviour and claiming to have witnessed "lights over the lake", Eliza has not been seen for three days. Men from Wintermoor have searched the surrounding lands and buildings, and dragged the lake without success. The search continues.

And the date on the newspaper was Saturday, 10th December 1864.

There it was. The pattern Tara was looking for. This had to mean something. She wanted to tell someone right away, so she pushed back her chair intending to go and find the librarian. But when she turned around, Tara saw, to her horror, that she was not alone in the room.

There were five people standing behind her in a line, blocking her escape.

Zoe, Jasmine, Jackie, Peter and Helen.

And they were all grinning.

Tara felt numb as she stared at the five figures standing in front of her. And the longer she stared at them, the more terrifying they became.

She noticed it in Zoe's face first. Her features faded, the way something faded when you stared at it for too long. It lost focus as if covered in a pale light. Her eyes disappeared to nothing, and her mouth was gone. Instead of a face, she was a confusing blur of light and colour. And when Tara looked at the others – Jackie, Jasmine, Peter and Helen – they were all the same.

As one, they stepped towards Tara. Her breath caught in her throat, and a sudden pain blazed through her head. It was like a red-hot needle slipping deep inside her brain. She wanted to scream, but she couldn't. She couldn't even breathe. Blinding panic coursed through her veins as she gagged for air, like a drowning girl clawing to reach the surface of the ocean. But she only sank deeper and deeper into the blackness.

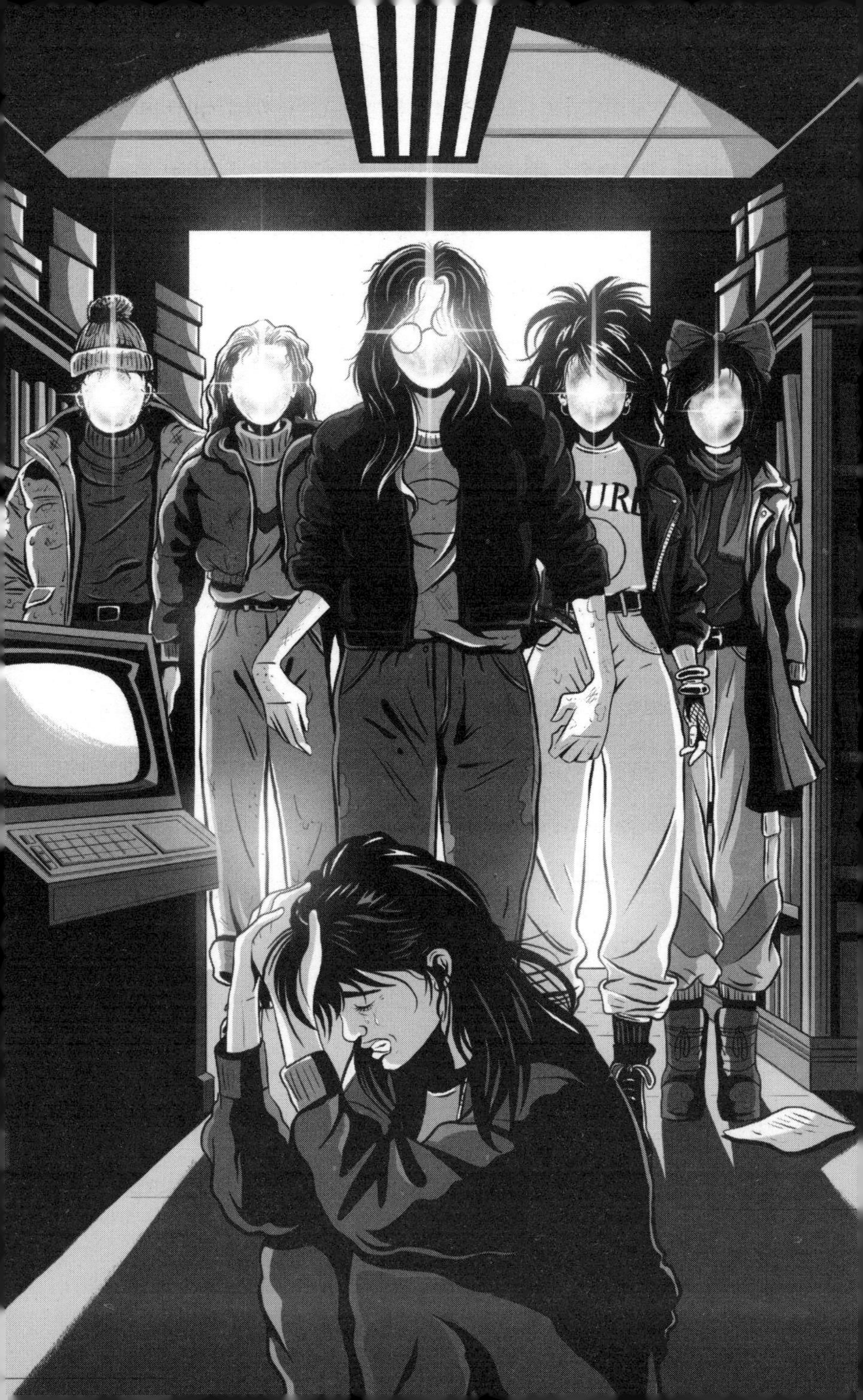

"Leave us alone," they said. "We are chosen."

But it didn't make sense that they were speaking – because their mouths were gone. How could they talk when they didn't have mouths? And why did it sound as if they spoke with a crowd of voices when there were only five of them?

This isn't real, Tara thought. *This isn't real.*

But it *was* real, and it was happening right now.

"We are chosen," they said again before they began to speak the numbers. Over and over. And every word was like another red-hot needle thrust into Tara's mind.

Tara put her hands to her head and fell to her knees. The world disappeared, and a tsunami of darkness crashed over her.

REPORT: X5N846-4

CLASSIFIED

T O P   S E C R E T

Interview with: Tara Fisher

Date: Friday, 9th January 1987

The following is taken from an interview with Tara Fisher that took place two years after the incident at Wintermoor.

TARA FISHER: If the librarian hadn't come in, I think they would've killed me or something.

NIGHT HOUSE AGENT: Really?

TARA FISHER: Well, yeah. I don't know how else to explain it – what was happening. What they were *doing* to me. I mean ... I couldn't breathe. My chest was tight, and it felt like someone was sticking hot nails in my brain. It must have been ESP – extrasensory perception – or tele-something.

NIGHT HOUSE AGENT: Telepathy?

TARA FISHER: Yeah. Exactly. Like in a film. I thought I was going to die.

NIGHT HOUSE AGENT: What did the librarian do? She didn't call the police?

TARA FISHER: The police already thought it was some kind of prank, so they weren't going to believe me, were they? I'd just get into trouble.

NIGHT HOUSE AGENT: And did you tell the librarian about your friends' faces? About what you saw? About what you think they did to you?

TARA FISHER: I told her everything. I mean,

she was the only person who thought I wasn't making it up. She was the only one who would actually listen to me.

NIGHT HOUSE AGENT: And you told her about the news articles?

TARA FISHER: Yes. I told her *everything*. Didn't I just say that? So, yeah, I told her about the articles, and that it was happening every forty years. That every forty years in December, kids went missing after seeing lights. And I told her about my friends in the garden and about the numbers and ... well, *everything*. But there was nothing she could do about it, was there? I couldn't prove anything, and nor could she.

NIGHT HOUSE AGENT: There was another incident the following week, wasn't there? On Wednesday, 12th.

TARA FISHER: You mean the assembly?

NIGHT HOUSE AGENT: Yes, the assembly. Can you tell us about that?

TARA FISHER: I gave you my diary, didn't I? It's in there, isn't it? Just read that.

Excerpt from TARA FISHER'S DIARY

Monday, 10th December 1984

On the way to school, I told Dennis what had happened at the library. About Zoe and them attacking me. I _think_ he believed me.

Anyway, when I told him about what I found in the newspapers, he said we should watch Zoe and Jasmine and see what happens. If it _is_ a prank, they'll get bored.

But I _know_ it isn't a prank because of what happened in the library. I didn't imagine it or make it up. I know how it felt and what they did to me and what they looked like. I mean, I can't even look at Zoe when I go into class because I'm so scared of her. I'm scared of my _best friend!_ And I'm scared that something really bad is going to happen.

I hardly even want to think it, but the librarian's friend disappeared in December 1944, and so did the boy from December 1904 and then the girl from December 1864. They all vanished after seeing the lights and acting weird. It's December 1984 now, exactly forty years on. So is that going to happen to Zoe and the others? What if they disappear too? And the worst thing is that none of the adults believe me.

Dennis says we should watch them to see what happens. If they try to run away or disappear or whatever, we'll see and we can tell someone. I don't know. I have a <u>really</u> bad feeling.

> Excerpt from TARA FISHER'S DIARY

Tuesday, 11th December 1984

I still can't look at Zoe and Jasmine, but I keep thinking about those newspapers from the library, and I'm scared something will happen to them. They <u>are</u> supposed to be my friends. Maybe they need help?

We followed Zoe home last night, and when her mum came to the door, Zoe just looked normal. But she <u>does</u> act normal most of the time. They <u>all</u> do. I've thought about it a lot and realised that the only time they act weird is when they think no one is watching. Or when I try to talk to them to find out what's wrong. Like they think I'm threatening them. So I'm keeping away.

Dennis and me went up to the music room to spy on them in the garden, and Sarah Jones from our year was already up there. She said her friend Paula is one of the "lights kids". That's what she called them: "lights kids".

Excerpt from TARA FISHER'S DIARY

Wednesday, 12th December 1984

We had a special assembly for the whole of Third Form today. When they told us to go to the hall, we all knew it had to be about what was happening. It's not just me and Dennis; <u>everyone</u> knows there's something weird going on.

We all know kids who go to the garden at lunch-time, and everyone has been talking about when they didn't turn up to school and were in the newspaper. Except no one talks about it when the "lights kids" are actually there because they might hear us, and we're all scared of them.

Not just me. <u>Everyone</u>. Even the teachers are different. Like they're shifty all the time. Maybe a bit scared like the rest of us. Anyway, when we were all sitting in the hall, Mr McNab came in with a policeman. They went up on the stage, and Mr McNab said he was getting sick and tired of "all this nonsense about lights in the sky" and stuff.

He said about all the bad behaviour - people doing graffiti, hanging about in the garden (which is out of bounds) and being mean and stuff. But then, right in the middle of him talking, a group of about twenty kids all stood up. The "lights kids". They all stood up, and the hall went <u>completely</u> silent. Mr McNab stopped talking, and it was, like, total silence. Then the "lights kids" started saying the numbers.

Oh my God, it was creepy. They just stared ahead and said the numbers. Mr McNab told them to stop, but they didn't, so he shouted, and the other teachers were trying to make them stop, but they just kept going, saying the numbers. Over and over.

They did it for maybe a whole minute before they suddenly stopped. Then they sat down all at the same time and acted like nothing had happened. But the worst thing was that when they were saying the numbers, they all looked like they did in the library and on the netball court. Their faces were gone. Completely gone. All I could see was like a weird light with all colours in it where they should have had faces. It's like they weren't real people any more.

REPORT: X5N846-5

CLASSIFIED

TOP SECRET

Interview with: Tara Fisher
Date: Friday, 9th January 1987

The following is taken from an interview with Tara Fisher that took place two years after the incident at Wintermoor.

NIGHT HOUSE AGENT: Did you tell anybody what you saw during the assembly? Did anybody else see the same thing?

TARA FISHER: Yeah. The other kids saw it.

NIGHT HOUSE AGENT: What about the teachers? And the policeman? Did they see their faces change?

TARA FISHER: I think they *couldn't* see it.

NIGHT HOUSE AGENT: Why do you think that?

TARA FISHER: Cos some of the kids tried to tell them what they saw, but they didn't believe them. So I think maybe it was something only kids could see.

NIGHT HOUSE AGENT: But everyone heard the children saying the numbers?

TARA FISHER: Yeah.

NIGHT HOUSE AGENT: Do you remember what the numbers were?

TARA FISHER: Not exactly. Not any more. But I think I did then. At the time.

NIGHT HOUSE AGENT: And they didn't mean anything to you?

TARA FISHER: Not right then. But ... yeah, later. In the night. That's when I realised what they meant.

Thursday, 13th December 1984

Tara hardly slept that Wednesday night. She couldn't stop thinking about what had happened in assembly. And when she *did* sleep, distorted faces invaded her dreams, and she heard numbers chanted by a thousand voices. She saw Jasmine turning to her, over and over again, her eyes blank as she whispered, "It's waking up. I am chosen."

In the early hours of the morning, she had an idea that forced her awake and turned her stomach. This idea filled her with a dark and heavy sense of foreboding. Something bad was going to happen. Something *catastrophic*.

She had to talk to Dennis about it.

Tara was up before her alarm even went off. She dressed quickly, got ready for school and went into the kitchen where her mum was making breakfast. But Tara couldn't eat anything because she thought it would just come back up again.

"You must have something," her mum said. "You can't go to school on an empty stomach. You won't be able to concentrate if you're—" But Tara wasn't listening. She had too many other things to worry about. So she grabbed a slice of toast to keep her mum quiet, then she left the flat.

As she walked to Dennis's house, she tore the toast into little pieces and dropped it in the snow for the birds. When it was gone, she dusted off her hands and jammed them into her pockets, keeping her head down. She had to see Dennis. She had to tell him her idea about what the kids had been saying in assembly. About the numbers. Except it wasn't numbers; it was *number*. One number. And it was getting smaller. It was one less every time the kids said it.

One hundred and thirty-nine thousand three hundred and five.

Then:

One hundred and thirty-nine thousand three hundred and four.

Then:

One hundred and thirty-nine thousand three hundred and three.

The number was some kind of countdown.

But to what?

She couldn't stop thinking about it. A countdown to what? What was going to happen when the countdown finished? She had to talk to Dennis about it. She had to tell him. Maybe he would know what it meant.

But when she came closer to Dennis's house and looked up, she felt as if the whole world was tilting sideways and she was going to fall off.

Because Dennis wasn't there.

He wasn't waiting outside his house like usual.

Tara had to *force* herself to put one foot in front of the other until she was standing at Dennis's front door.

"Please," she mumbled to herself. "Please, please, please. Not Dennis. Not Dennis."

She had to unclench her fist and make herself lift her hand to press the doorbell with one trembling finger.

"Please," she whispered. "Please, please, pl—"

The door opened and there stood Dennis's mum.

"Oh. Tara." She looked confused. "Er ... Dennis left already. He said he wanted to get to school early today."

Tara opened her mouth like a goldfish, then closed it again.

"Is everything all right?" Dennis's mum asked. "He seemed odd. Is it something to do with this silly prank at school? Dennis has been acting strangely since last night."

Tara wasn't listening any more. She was backing away from the door, shaking her head. The world was tipping and folding around her, and she suddenly felt as if she wasn't even inside her own body.

They got Dennis, was all she could think. *They got Dennis.*

"Are you all right?" Dennis's mum was saying. "Tara? Do you want me to call your mum? Is something wrong?"

Tara just shook her head and turned away, stumbling out onto the pavement and heading for school. She quickened her pace so she was almost running because she was desperate to see Dennis. She feared the worst but was hoping for the best. Maybe he'd needed to talk to one of the teachers, or maybe he'd had some homework to finish in the library, or ... *maybe he'd seen the lights. Maybe they'd got to him too ...*

No. No. Just the thought of it was too horrible.

Tara hurried to school and pushed past the other kids hanging around the gates. She headed into the main building without stopping. Tara ran along the corridor, ignoring Mr Straub's shouts for her to slow down, then she took the stairs two at a time to the second floor. She ran straight to her form room and stopped in the doorway.

Zoe, Jasmine, Jackie and all the "lights kids" were sitting at the back of the class, as they always did now. The other kids sat apart from them, separated by a whole row of empty tables so they didn't get too close.

Dennis wasn't at his usual table. He was sitting at the back.

"No," Tara said, and everyone in the room turned to look at her. "Not you, Dennis. Please. Not you."

Zoe grinned at her. "Dennis is with us now," she said. "He is chosen."

"Chosen for what?" Tara shouted. She couldn't help herself. "Chosen for what? Why are you doing this?"

The kids at the front of the class – the "non-lights kids" – suddenly sat up in their seats, interested to see what was going to happen. But the "lights kids" all stood up together. Their chairs scraped on the floor like fingernails on a chalkboard.

They turned to look at Tara.

"Stop it!" Tara shouted at them. She could feel herself losing control now. If they had wanted to drive her mad, it was working. "Chosen for what?"

"We are chosen," they said together. "We are chosen."

And then they began the countdown.

"Fifty-six thousand eight hundred and twenty-three.

"Fifty-six thousand eight hundred and twenty-two.

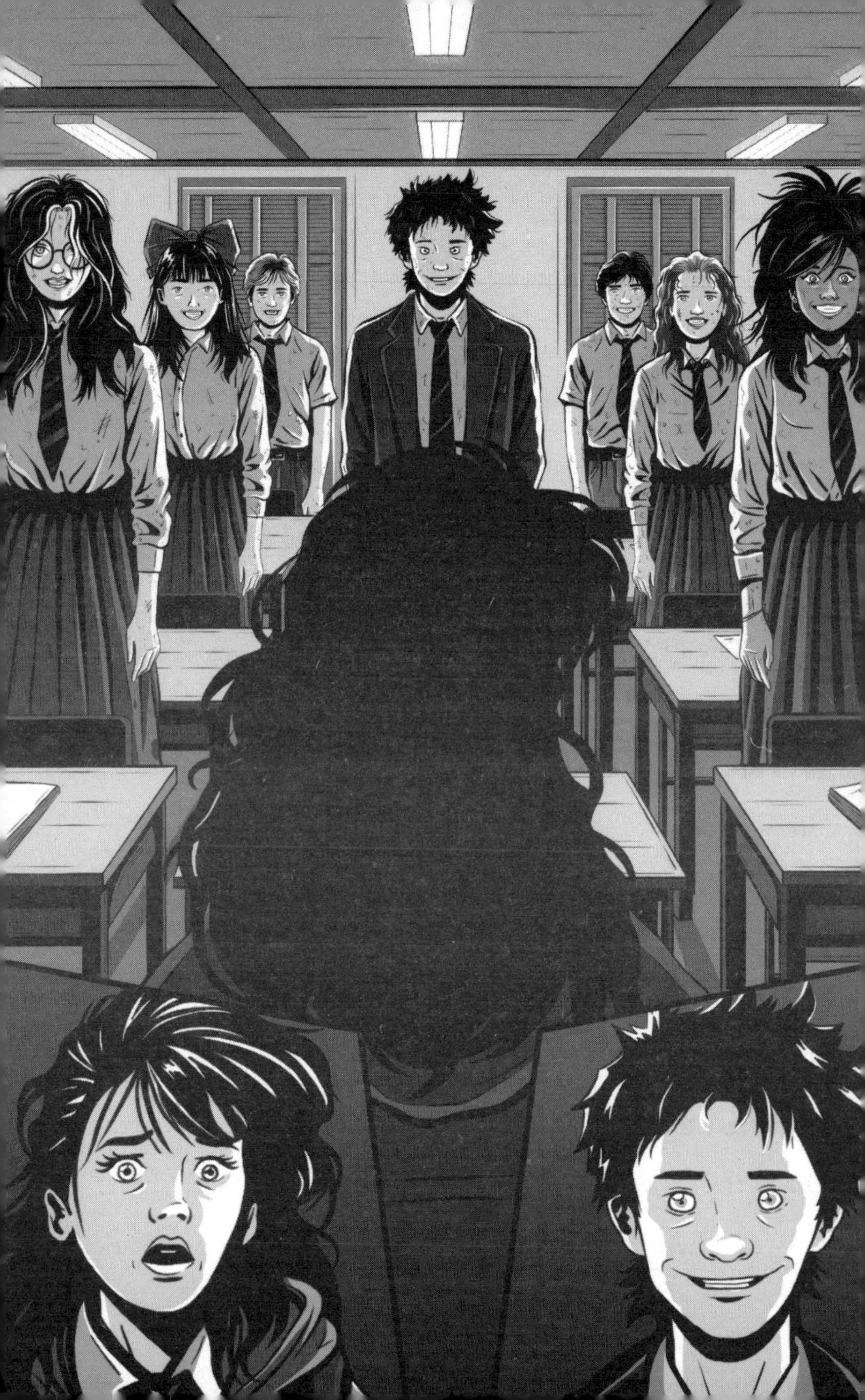

"Fifty-six thousand eight hundred and twenty-one."

"What does it mean?" Tara screamed at them. "What does it mean?!"

"What on earth is going on?" Miss James said, coming into the classroom behind Tara. "What's all this screaming about? I thought Mr McNab made himself clear. This has gone on for long enough!"

"It's them." Tara turned to Miss James. "It's them. The lights and the numbers and the staring. They're not real, Miss. They're not real. There's something wrong with them." Tara knew she was babbling. She knew she was losing control, but she couldn't stop herself. She couldn't hold it in any more.

"It's them!" She turned back to face the class and pointed, but Zoe and the others were all sitting in their seats now, looking at Tara with shock in their eyes. As if they were afraid of her. As if it was *Tara* that was the problem.

"I think perhaps you should come to Mr McNab's

office," Miss James said. "I'm surprised at you, Tara, causing such a fuss. This has to stop."

Tara pushed past Miss James and ran out into the corridor. She had to get away. She had to get as far away from there as possible.

Miss James shouted after Tara, bringing other teachers to their classroom doors to see what was going on. But Tara didn't listen to Miss James or anyone else who tried to stop her. She was blinded by tears and anger and confusion. She ran along the corridor, down the stairs and straight for the school entrance. The receptionist watched as Tara burst through the doors and ran out into the snow.

Tara didn't know where she was going. She ran until her legs burned, then she slowed to a walk. She wondered if she should go to the library. The librarian had been so kind to her, and it would be warm there. But she didn't want to see anyone or talk to anyone, so she made her way home and let herself in the front door.

Tara's mum was working in the shop, so it was cold and quiet in the flat. Like a graveyard.

Tara kicked off her shoes and went straight to her room. She lay on her bed and wrapped her duvet around herself, trying to feel warm and safe.

She must have fallen asleep because she woke when her mum came into her room.

"Tara? Are you all right? What are you doing here? School called and said something happened. Are you OK?"

Tara opened her eyes and blinked away her confusion. Mum must have closed the shop and come to see if she was at home.

"I'm fine, Mum," Tara managed. "Just ... really tired."

Her mum came to sit on the bed. She stroked a hand through Tara's hair. "What happened, my darling? Is it this prank thing?"

"I don't want to talk about it," Tara told her. "Please. I'm *so* tired. Just let me stay at home today.

Please. Tell school it's OK. Don't make me go back. Not today."

Tara's mum continued to stroke her hand through Tara's hair as she thought about it.

"All right," she said eventually. "You can stay here. Get some sleep. But we have to talk about this."

"Later," Tara said. "Please. Not now."

"OK," her mum agreed. "But I'll be right here if you need me. The shop can stay shut for one day. We'll survive."

"Thanks, Mum. Love you."

Tara slept until early evening. She hadn't realised how tired she was. When her mum came to check on her just after five o'clock, Tara was awake. Her mum wanted to talk to her, but Tara wanted to be left alone. So she stayed in her room and listened to music. She flicked through the handful of books she owned and wrote in her diary.

At around six o'clock, her mum made fish-finger sandwiches and tried to persuade Tara to come and watch TV while they ate, but Tara still wasn't ready. So her mum reluctantly left her to eat alone in her bedroom, making Tara promise to talk about it tomorrow.

Eventually, her mum went to bed and the flat fell silent.

Wintermoor fell silent around it.

Tara wrapped her duvet over her shoulders and stood at the window, watching the street. A few gentle snowflakes drifted from the sky, glimmering in the orange glow of the streetlights. Everything looked so normal, but Tara could sense that something was out there. She could feel it as strongly as if it were scratching at the door, begging to be let in.

And then, not long before midnight, the final horror began.

And it started with a familiar face.

When Tara noticed the bicycle coming along the street, she leaned closer to the window for a better look. She was surprised to see that it was a kid, maybe about her age. She couldn't tell whether it was a boy or girl because they were wearing jeans and a blue ski-jacket with the hood pulled up. But, more importantly, why were they out so late at night?

The bicycle passed, and a few seconds later, another bicycle approached from the same direction. This time, Tara recognised the rider straight away. She would have recognised that coat anywhere. It was Dennis.

Tara wasn't sure what surprised her most. Seeing Dennis out this late at night or seeing him on a bicycle. She didn't know he even owned one.

She was almost tempted to open the window and call to him, but she remembered what had happened this morning at school and stopped herself. Instead, she stayed silent and watched Dennis approach. He came at a steady pace along the middle of the road until he was almost level with Tara's flat. Then he stopped beneath the streetlight and turned to look directly up at Tara's window.

And he grinned.

Tara backed away quickly. Her room was in darkness, so Dennis couldn't have seen her ... could he?

Tara stayed in the shadows and watched Dennis sitting on his bike in the middle of the quiet road, under the streetlight. He stared up at her window with that ghastly grin on his face. And as Tara watched him, his features faded and blurred. They were being erased right in front of her eyes and replaced with an eerie, twisting glow. The pulsing light was stronger now than she had ever seen it.

After what felt like a long time, the light disappeared. It went away in an instant, and Dennis jerked as if he had woken from a dream about falling. The grin fell from his face and was replaced by a look of absolute terror. He turned his head like he was trying to figure out where he was and how he'd got there.

In that moment, Tara realised that something was controlling Dennis. Whatever it was, Dennis had managed to push it away, but only for a fraction of a second. Then there was a flicker of light in Dennis's eyes as he sat up straight and the awful grin returned.

He stared at Tara for a moment longer before he pushed off and cycled away into the night.

Then Tara went after him.

Tara quickly pulled on jeans and a jumper. She crept past her mum's bedroom to the end of the hall, then down the stairs. She was careful to avoid the third and seventh steps because they made a noise like someone standing on a cat.

At the bottom of the stairs, she grabbed her

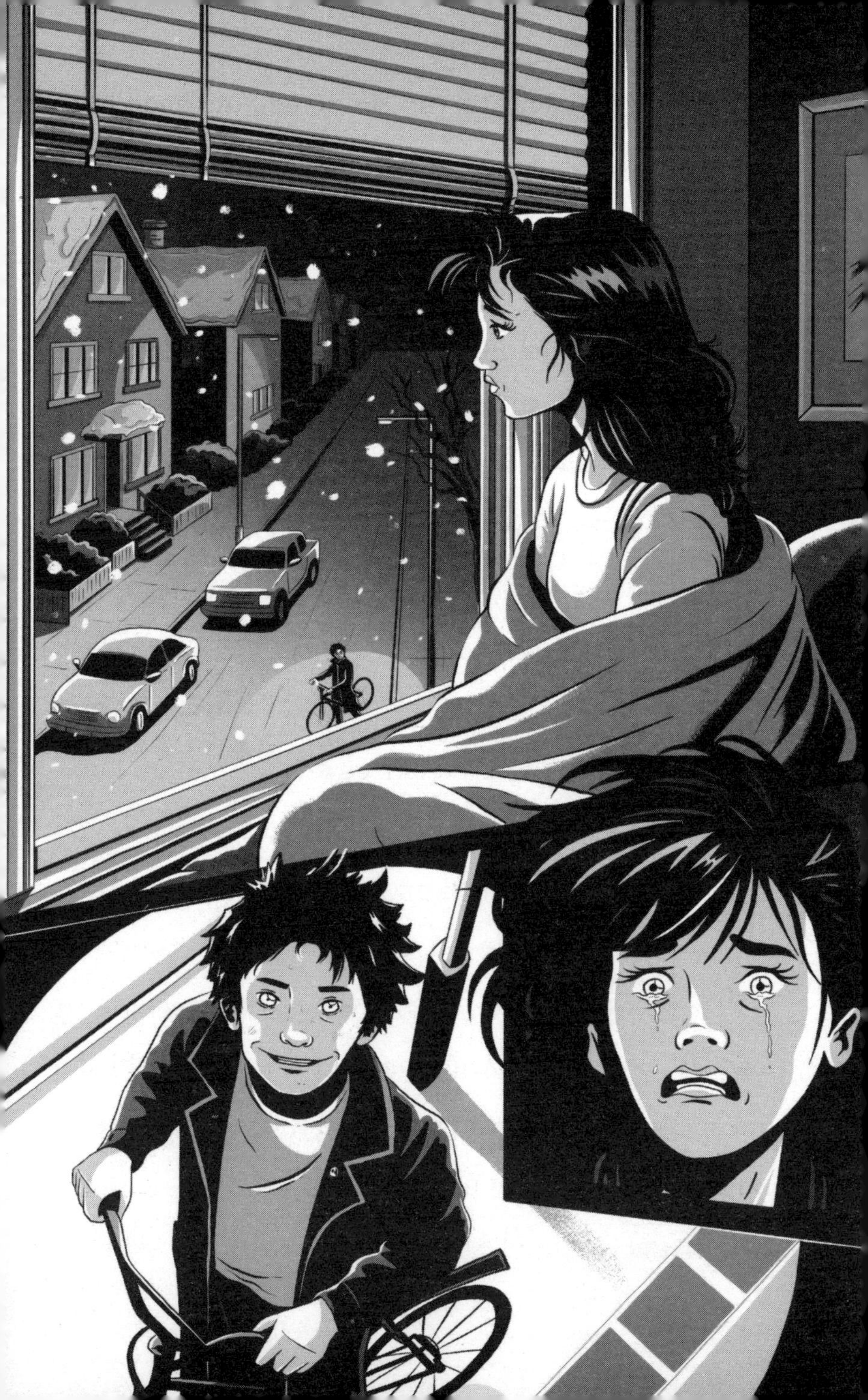

coat, jammed her feet into her trainers and eased open the front door. She wheeled out Mum's old "Antiques" bicycle and closed the front door without making a sound.

Mission accomplished.

She took the bike onto the road, wondering if it would still work or if the rusty chain would fall off. But when she mounted it, the pedals were firm, and the chain worked perfectly as she set off in the direction Dennis had gone.

The road was icy, and the snowfall was growing heavier. Flakes caught on her eyelashes and on her lips. Her face and hands were numb after just a couple of minutes, and she wished she had brought a hat and gloves.

Tara braked at the end of the street, looking left and right, but there was no sign of Dennis.

Then Tara spotted a bicycle track in the fresh snow. It curved right, bumping up onto the pavement and then back down again.

It had to be Dennis.

Tara set off again, cycling faster, and after a minute or two she spotted him ahead. He was moving in and out of the streetlights as he progressed along the road.

Tara kept her distance. She didn't want Dennis to spot her.

At the end of the road, Dennis went straight over onto the next street, then diagonally across the park. About halfway across the park, close to the children's play area, someone else on a bicycle appeared from his left. Tara couldn't be sure, but she thought it might be Jack Martin from school.

He came out of the darkness, cycling across the grass, on a collision course with Dennis. But at the last moment, Jack suddenly turned so he was cycling beside Dennis. The two of them crossed the park side by side and left through the gates at the far end.

Tara followed, but as soon as she reached the gates, she brought her bike to a sudden stop.

There were more kids from school on the street beyond the park. Jasmine, Helen and Connor Benchley were walking in a group just by the park entrance. Another three kids on bikes were following close behind Dennis and Jack.

Tara was afraid to approach them or get too close. She didn't want them to attack her like they had before, so she waited in the shadows for them to get ahead before she followed.

At the end of the street, another group of four kids appeared from a side road to join them. They walked in step, all moving at the same speed.

Tara climbed off her bike and wheeled it as she followed them out of town.

―

Tara's hands were numb even though she had pulled down her coat sleeves to cover them. Her toes were freezing too. As she left the town behind her, the sky cleared to reveal a pale half-moon. The road was thick with snow, and the fields on either side glinted in the moonlight. If it weren't for the situation, Tara might have thought it was a beautiful night.

The group of kids kept walking until they reached Wintermoor Woods, then they turned and disappeared into the trees.

Tara stopped, glancing over her shoulder to make sure there weren't any others behind her, then she slowly approached the spot where the kids had entered the woods.

There, she found a collection of abandoned bicycles – perhaps nine or ten of them lying in the snow at the side of the road. Close by, there was a trail of footprints leading into the trees.

Tara lay down her bike, stuffed her hands into her pockets and followed the trail.

Slowly, she moved deeper into the woods. There was no sign of the other kids, just their footprints lit by the faint glow of moonlight that spilled through the gnarly, leafless treetops. She trudged deeper and deeper into the trees, and as she came closer to the lake, her sense of dread deepened.

It wasn't the cold that was making her bones ache now. It was fear. The most intense and solid fear she had ever experienced. It gripped every part of her in its cold, cold fingers, and it squeezed.

But she pressed on until finally she stepped out of the trees and into the large clearing in the centre of the woods. And there, surrounded by the watchful trees, was Wintermoor Lake, its surface frozen to a sheet of thin ice.

Usually, this was a fun and exciting place to be. In the summer, Tara would come here with her friends. They would lie in the sun by the water. They would play games, have picnics or walk the colour-coded routes that criss-crossed the woods.

But on the night of Thursday, 13th December 1984, what she found in the clearing was a nightmare.

All of the "lights kids" from school were there. At least twenty of them, including her friends

Zoe, Jasmine and Dennis. They were spread out at the edge of the lake, standing with their heads tilted towards the sky as if they were waiting for something.

And then they began to speak.

———

It was an eerie and terrifying thing to see. All of the kids stood motionless in the night, staring upwards, speaking to the sky. In front of them, the lake was frozen over, reflecting the glow of the half-moon that watched from the black canvas above. A smattering of stars shimmered. The twisted, naked branches of the surrounding trees waited, creaking gently in the breeze.

Tara stood at the edge of those trees and tilted her head to listen to what the kids were mumbling.

She couldn't quite make out the words, but she *knew* what they would be. She knew. But even though she knew, she wanted to hear. She *had* to hear. So she stepped from the shadow of the trees and into the moonlight. She crept closer to the kids at the edge of the lake until she could hear clearly.

"One hundred and nineteen.

"One hundred and eighteen.

"One hundred and seventeen."

Tara's heart thudded in her chest as if it might crack through her ribs. They were saying the number, and it was becoming ever smaller. She was now *certain* that it was a countdown, and that it was reaching its end. She was also certain that whatever was going to happen, it was not going to be good, and she was the only person who could do anything to stop it.

"No!" She screamed the word before she even knew she was going to. "Stop!"

The kids by the lake didn't react. They just stood and stared and continued their countdown.

"Ninety-nine. Ninety-eight. Ninety-seven."

"Please! Stop!" Tara broke into a run, her

trainers slip-sliding on the snow as she hurried towards the lake edge.

"Zoe! Dennis!" She screamed the names of her friends. "Jasmine!"

No one reacted. It was like Tara wasn't even there.

"Stop it! You have to stop!" Tara pleaded as she closed the distance, reaching the semicircle of kids by the lake with their faces turned towards the sky.

She went straight to Dennis because he was closest. She grabbed his arm, but when she pulled him, his arm didn't budge. She tugged harder, but he remained rigid, with his arms by his side, as if he were made of stone.

Tara tried again, but Dennis didn't move, so she let go and looked around in fear and desperation. She spotted Zoe, with Jasmine standing beside her. Helen was there, and Jackie and Connor and Jack, and all the other kids from school who had been acting strangely.

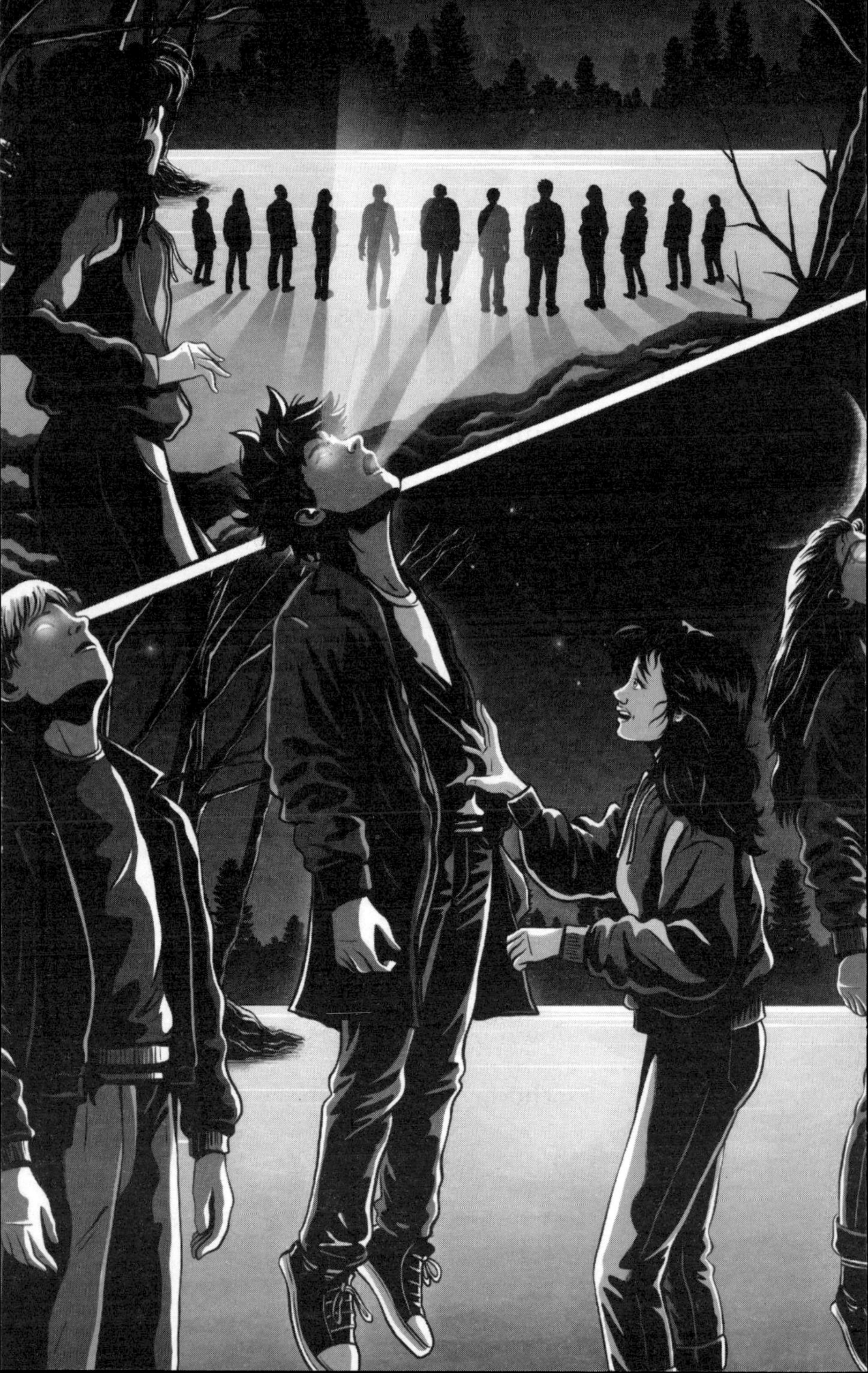

"What are you all doing?" Tara screamed before turning her attention back to Dennis, who simply continued to count down.

"Twenty-two. Twenty-one. Twenty. Nineteen."

Whatever was coming, it was close. There was almost no time left. Just seconds.

Tara moved round in front of Dennis, trying to get his attention. He continued to stare skywards, his face blank, but when Tara looked right into his eyes, she saw a strange light there. The light grew brighter, as if it were rising from somewhere deep inside him. A glow began to cover his face, making his features fade into nothing. And then Tara had the strangest sense that Dennis was growing taller.

No, he wasn't growing taller.

He was ... how was it possible?

Tara looked down and saw that Dennis's feet were no longer on the ground but floating above it and rising higher.

"N ... no." Tara stepped back in horror. Her heel

cracked the thin ice at the edge of the lake, and the freezing water seeped into her trainer.

"Ten. Nine. Eight." The kids continued to count down, and now all of them had the same glow around their faces. And they were all rising above the ground, floating out across the water, like puppets on strings.

"Please." Tara's voice was quiet now. The fight had gone out of her. Her whole body trembled as she turned to watch the kids come together and hover over the centre of the lake. Their bodies were smothered in glowing light.

"Three."

"Two."

"One."

Tara's strength abandoned her, and she fell to her knees in the frozen mud. All she could do was watch as the icy surface of the lake cracked, and the black water began to boil. It bubbled and frothed angrily, while a silky, oily steam seeped upwards, coiling around the feet of the kids hovering above it.

At the same time, the kids tipped their heads right back as the glow forced its way up and out of them. Their throats bulged, their eyes streamed and their mouths opened wider than Tara would ever have thought possible. The glow emerged from each of them as a solid, shining, living thing. An almost spherical shape that rippled and pulsed with all the colours of the rainbow. One light for each of them. The glowing shapes rose above the floating children – slowly, slowly – then, in a flash, they darted down into the boiling black water.

Immediately, the lake lit up as if it had come to life. Colours flashed in the depths in a mesmerising display of light. Black, watery tentacles erupted from its surface, twisting and coiling as they tested the air. The tentacles probed upwards, reaching for the children hovering over the water.

What Tara was seeing was impossible, and yet there it was. The lake was alive. A dormant

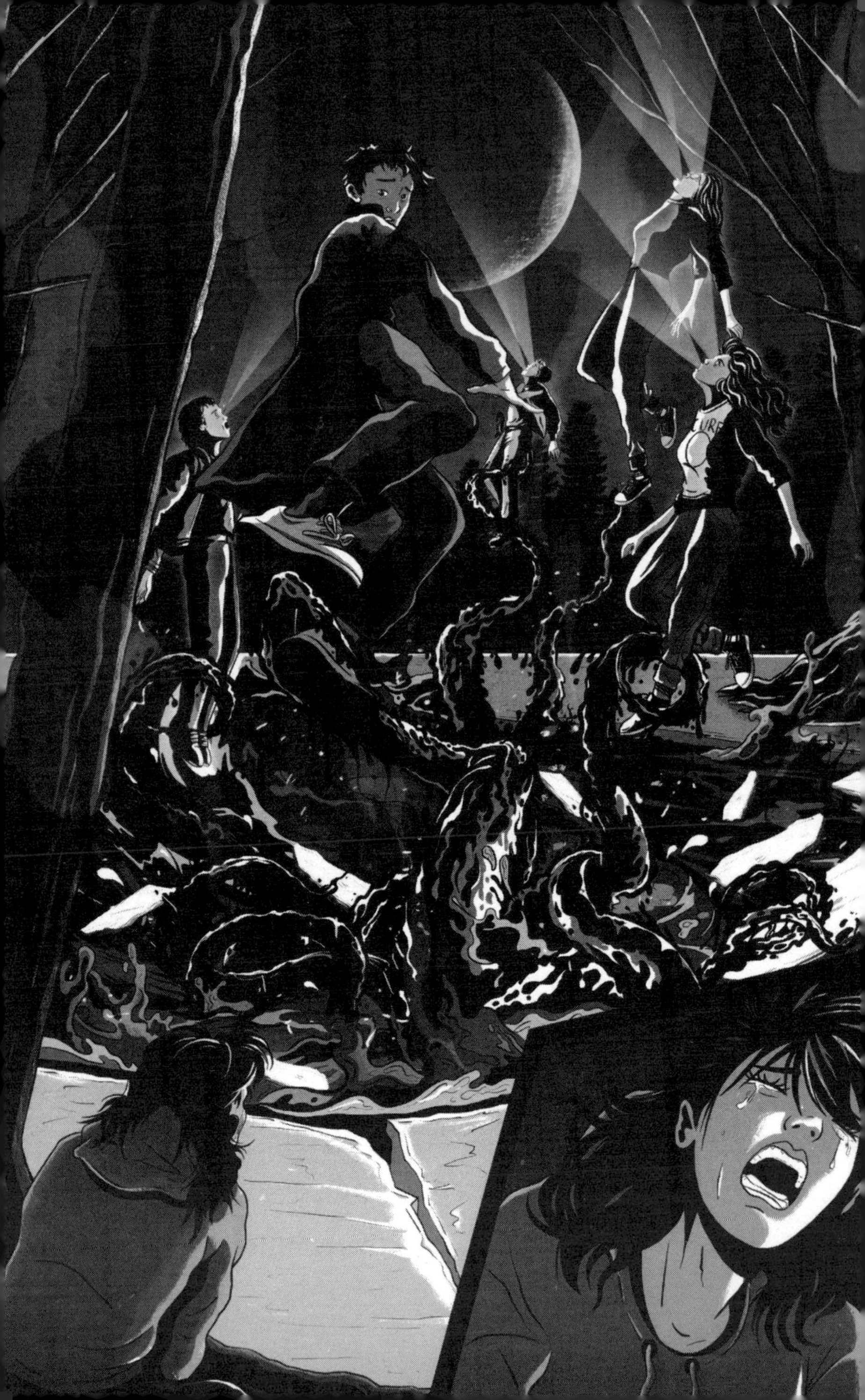

creature had suddenly and violently woken. Tara was both awestruck and terrified by the incredible display of light and life. But of all the things that could go through her mind, the only thing she could think was that no one would ever believe what she had seen.

Tara could only watch in horror as the watery tentacles slipped around the feet of the hovering children and coiled about their legs. Tara watched them wrap around Dennis's body, covering him almost entirely as if encasing him in tar, until all that was visible of him was his head. Then Tara noticed something that would stay with her always. An image that would forever be burned into her memory.

Dennis was looking straight at her, his eyes wide in terror and confusion.

The light had left him, and he was Dennis again, awake and afraid.

But time had run out.

"Help m—" he began to say, but with sudden and brutal speed, the tentacles jerked back down into the lake, dragging Dennis and all the other children down into the water.

One moment Dennis and the others were there. The next moment they were gone.

Then the lights faded, the surface of the lake settled and it was over.

Tara was left alone in the night.

Interview with Tara Fisher
Date: Tuesday, 2nd April 2024

Along with the contents of File Number ET339, the Nightwatchman included a note with a telephone number on it. My instruction was to call the number after I had read the file. When I did, I found myself speaking with Tara Fisher herself.

The following is part of the transcript of the conversation I had with Tara during that telephone call on 2nd April 2024, nearly forty years after the event she claims to have experienced. I tried to call the number a second time, but it had been disconnected.

TARA FISHER: My friends were gone. All of them. They went down into the lake, and they were gone. I didn't make it up. I know what I saw.

DAN SMITH: And the lake was—

TARA FISHER: Calm. I remember it so clearly. The lake was calm, like nothing had happened. But it *did* happen. I even went right to the edge and looked in, but it was just water. Except my friends had gone in there. All of them. And no one ever saw them again. I went home and told my mum, and she called the police. The police went up to the lake and found all the bikes, but no one believed me when I told them what I had seen. I mean, of course they didn't; it was ridiculous. Everyone thought I was lying – that it was all part of some stupid game. They thought everyone would turn up the next day. But of course they didn't, so the police dragged the lake. When they didn't find anything there, they started saying it was some kind of cult and that all the kids had run away. It was a thing back then, you know? People were afraid their children would be brainwashed by a cult and kidnapped. So that was the answer they came up with. And people thought I knew more than I was saying, so first Zoe's mum and dad begged me to tell them where Zoe had gone. Then Dennis's parents and Jasmine's. Then all the parents were ringing and coming to the flat or the shop. It was awful. People in the town started saying I had done something or that I knew something, and they harassed me to the point where I couldn't go to school any more. And I became obsessed with the lake. With my friends going missing. I would sneak out at night and go there, just stand by the water in the freezing cold. The whole thing made me ill eventually, so in the end Mum sold the shop and we left Wintermoor for good.

DAN SMITH: Could you have been mistaken about what you saw? Could it have been some kind of hallucination? Maybe some kind of gas coming out of the lake?

TARA FISHER: Gas? No. I know what I saw. I've had a long time to think about it.

DAN SMITH: So what do you think happened? How do you *explain* what you saw?

TARA FISHER: How do I explain it? What do I think? I think it was alive.

DAN SMITH: You think the lake was alive?

TARA FISHER: Yes. It wasn't water. It was something else. Something alive. Or at least something that came to life every forty years to feed. I think the lights were part of it – they came out of the lake and went into my friends. The lights slowly took them over and then brought them to the lake at the right time. When it was ready to feed. There are other creatures in nature that do similar things. Hairworms infect crickets and use them to hitch a ride to bodies of water like lakes so the crickets jump in, drown and the hairworms can get into the water to reproduce. Fungi and flatworms can infect ants' brains and control them.

DAN SMITH: But something coming out of the lake and controlling children? You know how that sounds, don't you?

TARA FISHER: Like I've lost my mind. I know. But I can't find any other explanation for it.

DAN SMITH: And why do you think it didn't take *you?*

TARA FISHER: I sometimes wish it had. But maybe I was the wrong age – the others were all fourteen. Even the kids who disappeared in the past – in 1944 and 1904 – were fourteen. But I was young for my school year, so maybe it was that? Or maybe it was just random. I'll probably never know.

DAN SMITH: I'm sorry. It must have been very difficult for you to lose so many friends and to have everyone think you were lying.

TARA FISHER: Someone believed me.

DAN SMITH: Really? What do you mean?

TARA FISHER: Back then. Someone believed me. Like I said, after the incident, I became obsessed with the lake. I couldn't keep away from it. The police cordoned off the whole area, but there were ways into the woods, so I went in there day and night to watch the water. I kept hoping I'd see something that would make sense. Or that my friends would just walk out of there or ... I don't know. I needed to make sense of it. But then one day, weeks later, after the police were gone and the barriers were taken down, I saw people there by the water. They had all this scientific equipment with them, as if they were testing the water. The next day, there were more of them, except now they were wearing protective suits. You know, like they were working with dangerous chemicals or some kind of disease. The day after that, they came and took it away.

DAN SMITH: The lake?

TARA FISHER: Yes, the lake. All of it. They closed off the whole road and put up signs saying they were resurfacing it, but I know the truth. They closed the road so no one would see what they were doing. But I saw. They brought tankers, a lot of them, and lined them up on the road by the woods. Then they fed these huge pipes into the lake and they drained it.

DAN SMITH: Are you serious?

TARA FISHER: Oh yes. They sucked up the whole lake and took it away. There's no lake there any more, just a great big hole in the middle of the woods. Go and have a look if you don't believe me. See for yourself.

NIGHT HOUSE FILE NUMBER ET339:
The Wintermoor Lights

Author's Conclusion

After speaking to Tara Fisher in that short and strange conversation, something she said stayed with me.

"Go and have a look if you don't believe me. See for yourself."

I couldn't stop thinking about that. I knew where Wintermoor was, and it wouldn't take more than a few hours for me to get there. So why not? Why not do as she suggested? Why *not* go and see it for myself?

So I did.

Wintermoor is not the real name of the town. I made that up, as per the Nightwatchman's wishes, so don't go looking for it. And don't ever ask me to reveal the real town's name because I would never do that.

I arrived there late one summer afternoon. The first thing that struck me about Wintermoor was how normal it seemed. It was like any other small town in the English countryside. Old and new houses, the church, the old library and a small high street of struggling shops. But when I passed through it and made my way towards the woods, I felt a chill of excitement. It was almost exactly as I had imagined it: the narrow country road with fields on one side and the woods on the other. It was as if I had been there before.

I parked my car in perhaps the same place that Tara had left her bicycle on that terrible night, and I stood for a moment. A warm breeze lifted across the fields, carrying smells from a distant farmyard. Then I searched for a good spot to climb the barbed-wire fence that now separates the woods from the road.

I discovered a sagging strand of wire, the barbs matted with sheep's wool, so I climbed over and headed into the trees.

At once, I felt my excitement shift and darken. I wasn't afraid exactly, but something like it. The air was still and cool in the shade of the woods. There was an inexplicable sense that terrible things had happened there. Something felt wrong. It was an unhappy place.

The lake itself was impossible to miss. Or I should say the place where the lake had once been. I came through the woods into a large clearing and saw it: a gaping crater surrounded by trees. If I'd ever had any doubts about what I had read in File Number ET339, they went away right then. In the forty years since Tara Fisher's story, nothing has grown in the lakebed. No trees, no bracken, no weeds, nothing. Not one single thing.

Wintermoor Lake is a black hole in the ground.

I didn't stay long. There was something

unwelcoming about that place, so I left and headed back into Wintermoor, where I had booked a room in a small B&B. The following morning, before I drove away from Wintermoor, I visited the library. I looked at the microfiche files Tara had looked at. They are still there, in the room where she claims she was attacked by Zoe and the others. Perhaps I even sat in the same seat Tara had sat in. No one had bothered to remove or hide the files. Why would they need to? No one ever believed Tara anyway.

As I write this, it is now just over forty years since the mass disappearance of children at Wintermoor. Thankfully the forty-year cycle was not repeated. No children disappeared from the town in December 2024.

―――

So what is the truth? Do we believe Tara Fisher's account? What *were* the Wintermoor lights? What *was* lurking in the woods? Why were the children acting so strangely, and where did they go?

The official story is that no one knows for sure what happened to the Wintermoor children. Perhaps they were kidnapped by a cult, perhaps they all ran away together or perhaps they were abducted by aliens. There have been many, many theories. But I think the truth is much stranger. I think it is exactly as Tara Fisher told it.

Night House agents investigated and confirmed that, in February 1985, government scientists did indeed come to test the waters of Wintermoor Lake. The results of those tests are classified as Top Secret, and, no matter how hard the Night House has tried, agents have been unable to see them.

Night House agents have also confirmed that the water from the lake at Wintermoor was removed. It was transported to a facility on a remote island several miles off the coast of Scotland. The island belongs to the British government and is heavily guarded. It does not appear on any map.

There, on the island, the contents of the lake are kept beneath a dome constructed of steel and concrete. In 1989, two Night House agents were able to access the dome, but only one of them made it back from the island. Since then, Night House agents have made several more attempts to access the island, but all have failed so far. The agent who successfully returned from the island in 1989 reported that inside the dome she had seen children "floating above the water before being dragged down". She was able to confirm that whatever is contained inside that dome of concrete and steel is not a lake. It is something else. Something "not of this Earth".

Investigations continue.

CLASSIFIED
THE HOUSE OF HORRORS

Coming soon ...

CLASSIFIED

TOP SECRET

THE HOUSE OF HORRORS

Released: May 2026

> Excerpt from article on mond0bizarro.com dated March 2022

What really happened at Coyote Creek?

Hey, truth-seekers, how about this for a weird little story? Between 2017 and 2020, thirty-two people were reported missing in and around a large area of the Chihuahuan desert in West Texas. For a long time, police were completely clueless. It was as if the people just disappeared off the face of the earth. Abducted by aliens, you might think. Or perhaps it was a new "Bermuda Triangle". Well, we still don't really know. But what we do know is that in July 2020, events led police to an abandoned town two miles from the lonely desert highway.

The town was called Coyote Creek.

So-called "ghost towns" aren't unusual in West Texas. Abandoned mining towns and other failed communities litter the harsh desert landscape. But Coyote Creek was hiding a dark secret. You see, in the middle of the town, among the broken and collapsing buildings, police discovered a large house. Inside that house, they found the "remains" of all those missing people. All thirty-two of them. The exact state of those "remains" has never been made public, but rumours tell of strange cults, outlandish waxworks and even the undead.

For a short time in July 2020, Coyote Creek was a hive of activity (see photos below). Police and federal investigators were on site for several days, and witnesses report seeing many vehicles entering and leaving the area.

But soon after the investigation was over, almost all records were lost in a fire. Everything went up in smoke like someone was trying to get rid of evidence. The house itself was demolished along with the rest of Coyote Creek, and now there is no trace of the town, or of what happened there.

The whole incident smells like a cover-up to us at mond0bizarro.com. There's an "official" version of events, but we just don't believe it. Something bizarre happened in that house; something that would make your hair stand on end. Government experiments maybe? A Satanic cult? Alien invaders? No one really knows for sure – except the people who were there and those who covered it up.

So, fellow conspirators, what do you think really happened in that old house in Coyote Creek? And why are the authorities covering it up? Put your answers in the comments.

THE NIGHT HOUSE FILES